IS THE MAGIC NUMBER
JP SAYLE

Other Books

Standalone
When Fake Changed Everything
Christmas beyond Christmas
The Elves and the Bondage Daddy (Grim and Sinister Delights Book 5)

Series
The Potters Creek Series
A Christmas Wish (book one)

The App Series
The App: Daddy kink (book one)
The App: Littles (book two)
The App: Puppy play (book three)

The Flamingo Bar Series
Always More (book one)
The Little Side of Me (book two)
3 is the magic number (book three)

La Trattoria Di Amore Series
Puzzle Pieces (book one)
Dominated but not Subdued (book two)

Sometimes you have to listen when you boys talk no matter where they take you. I hope you enjoy where Bailey, Jake and Sam traveled.

The books come with a lot of support, my Manx Minx's, Tina, Mandy, Julie, Abbie, Guy and as always you have my eternal thanks and love.

Can close proximity provide Jake, Bailey, and Sam the chance to find out if three is the magic number?

Jake's search for love, the one thing that has been missing from his life, leads him to not one, but two men. With everything at stake, does he have what both Sam and Bailey need?

Sam finds that sometimes the past chooses not to stay where it belongs. He must decide if Jake's promises can give him something he craves: unconditional love.

Hiding from his past causes ripples that create a backlash, leaving Bailey facing some hard truths. Will the past be too hard to overcome, or will Sam and Jake's love change everything?

3 Is the Magic Number is the third in the Flamingo Bar series. It is an MMM, close proximity, hurt/comfort romance with angst and a steam factor. This book is the duet to The App: Puppy Play, the third book in the App series, and the author recommends that book should be read first.

Book Character Family Tree

Below are the characters that can be found in other books and series written or being written.

Bailey — (Ex Army Sergeant, partner Sam and Jake)—Main Character The App: Puppy Play (book 3) The App Series, 3 Is the Magic Number, (Book 3) The Flamingo Bar Series. In Part Three Mine Body and Soul: The Playroom Series, Ferron's Journey Part Two: Hidden & Part Three: Revelation, The Playroom Series (Books 5 & 6)

Jake — (Architect, partner Sam and Bailey)— Main Character The App: Puppy Play (book 3) The App Series, 3 Is the Magic Number, (Book 3) The Flamingo Bar Series. In The Playroom Series books 1-6.

Sam — (Bar Manager Flamingo Bar, partner Jake and Bailey)— Main Character The App: Puppy Play (book 3) The App Series, 3 Is the Magic Number, (Book 3) The Flamingo Bar Series. In The Playroom Series books 5&6, The Flamingo Bar Series book 2, The App Series book 2.

Sawyer — (Waiter in LTDA, partner Boyd)—Main Character The App: Littles (book 2) The Little Side of Me, (book 2) The Flamingo Bar. In The App: Daddy Kink, (book 1), La Trattoria Di Amore Series book 1 &2, The Playroom Series books 1-6.

Boyd — (Construction Owner, partner Sawyer)— Main Character The App: Littles (book 2) The Little Side of Me, (book 2) The Flamingo Bar. In Mine, Body and Soul Trilogy: The Playroom Series, The Playroom Series books 1-6.

Isaac — (Bar Manager of The Playroom, Ferron's partner)— Main Character Ferron's Journey Part One: Damaged, (Book 4), Ferron's Journey Part Two: Hidden (Book 5) Ferron's Journey Part Three: Revelation, (Book 6) The Playroom Series. In Dominated but not Subdued: La Trattoria Di Amore Series (book 2), Mine, Body and Soul: The Playroom Series books 1-3. The App series 1-3, The Flamingo Bar Series 1-3.

Ferron — (Bartender in The Playroom, Isaac's partner)— Main Character Ferron's Journey Part One: Damaged, (Book 4), Ferron's Journey Part Two: Hidden (Book 5) Ferron's Journey Part Three: Revelation, (Book 6) The Playroom Series. In La Trattoria Di Amore series book 1&2, Mine, Body and Soul: The Playroom Series books 1-3. The App series 1-3, The Flamingo Bar Series 1-3.

Scott — (Waiter in LTDA, partner Luke)—Main Character The App: Daddy Kink, Always More, Flamingo Bar Series. In La Trattoria Di Amore Series (book 1&2), The Playroom Series books 1-6. The App series 2-3, The Flamingo Bar Series 2-3.

Luke — (Hotel Manager)—Main Character in The App: Daddy Kink, Always More, The Flamingo bar, (book 1). In The Manx Cat Guardians Series, (book 6 & 7), Property of a Billionaire, (book one) Billionaire's Playground.

Adam — (Floor Manager of LTDA, partner Carl)— Main Character Dominated but not Subdued: La Trattoria Di Amore, (book 2). In La trattoria Di Amore book 1, The Playroom Series books 1-6. The App series 1-3, The Flamingo Bar Series 1-3. Billionaire's Playground

Carl — (Head Chef of LTDA and Co-owner of The Playroom, partner Adam)—Main Character Dominated but not Subdued: La Trattoria Di Amore, (book 2). In La Trattoria Di Amore Series (book 1),Mine, Body and Soul Trilogy, The App: Daddy Kink (book 1)

Nathan — (Co-owner of The Playroom, partner Lenny)— Main Character Mine, Body and Soul Trilogy, Playroom Series books 1-3. In The Playroom series books 4-6, La Trattoria Di Amore Series (book 1 & 2), The App series 1-3, The Flamingo Bar Series 1-3.

Lenny — (Trainee Chef of LTDA, partner Nathan)—Main Character Mine, Body and Soul Trilogy, Playroom Series books 1-3. In The Playroom series books 4-6, La Trattoria Di Amore Series (book 1 & 2), The App series 1-3, The Flamingo Bar Series 1-3.

Brett — (Psychologist, partner to Guy)—Main Character Reluctant Billionaire, (book 2) Billionaire's Playground. In Billionaire's Playground (book 1), The Flamingo Bar, book 1.

Guy— (Student, partner to Guy)—Main Character Reluctant Billionaire, (book 2) Billionaire's Playground. In Billionaire's Playground (book 1), The Flamingo Bar, book 1.

Griffin — (Tycoon, partner to Charlie)—Main Character Property of a Billionaire. In The Flamingo Bar Series, book 1, Billionaire's Playground Series book 2.

Charlie — (Student, partner to Griffin)—Main Character Property of a Billionaire. In The Flamingo Bar Series, book 1, Billionaire's Playground Series book 2.

Richie — (Office assistant LTDA, partner Seb)—Main Character La Trattoria Di Amore Series (book 1). In La Trattoria Di Amore, (book 2), In The Playroom series books 1-6, The App series 1-3.

Sebastian — (Co-owner of LTDA restaurants with Carl, partner Richie)—Main Character La Trattoria Di Amore Series (book 1). In La Trattoria Di Amore, (book 2), Mine, Body and Soul Trilogy, The App: Daddy Kink (book 1), The Manx Cat Guardians (book 7)

Theo — (Waiter in LTDA)—La Trattoria Di Amore Series (book 1&2), Mine, Body and Soul Trilogy: The Playroom Series. Ferron's Journey Part One: Damaged, The Playroom Series (book 4), The Flamingo Bar (book 3), The App Series, book 2.

Chapter One

Bailey

Outside the door to The Playroom, I stared up at the building, not quite sure how I'd got there after leaving Jake's house. I wasn't sure how much time had passed since I'd found Jake and Sam playing together. Considering what happened after I'd gone into the room and been faced with Sam's pain and Jake's questions; it wasn't nearly enough.

A shiver ran over my skin, despite the warmth of the day. The sky was deep-blue with fluffy white clouds, a picture of serenity. It reminded me of days when I'd found peace in submission, when I'd understood what I needed, what I wanted from life. It seemed I'd lost sight of that, and in the process, I'd fucked everything up at every turn, making it my mission to worsen an already impossible situation. Unable to see any way to fix things, that's definitely how it felt.

Right now, I felt as if I were submerged in water with something tied to my feet, weighing me down. It was stopping me from getting to the surface, from taking a breath. And if it continued, I wasn't sure I'd ever be able to find my way back, and that scared me more than anything.

I cracked my knuckles as I eyed the door warily, knowing without a doubt that Nathan would make me face the hard truths.

What did I want? The easy answer was Sam, but it was also the complicated answer too. When Nathan had suggested reaching out to Sam and talking about what we could do to make things work between us with a third, it had all seemed so simple. But only if I didn't consider the way I'd left things with him, that I'd never been honest about myself, or how I'd feel towards Jake being with Sam. I wanted to submit to Jake, but I also wanted to punch his lights out for having the connection with Sam that I'd dreamed about.

Sam had been right to call me a coward. That's exactly what I was, and the situation was a big, fucked-up mess. All of it was a mind fuck, and I needed to talk to someone before I burst a blood vessel.

Inhaling, I let the air fill my chest, hoping it would ease the band that had formed around my upper body the second I'd walked out of Jake's home and away from...what?

A chance at the life you've always dreamed of?

I didn't dream of being in a relationship with two men!

That may be the case but look at what it could offer you.

What, the green-eyed monster?

That was just the shock, think about it.

I stood as the voices in my head argued back and forth for so long, the door in front of me opened to reveal Lenny. He was dressed for the warm weather in brightly coloured shorts and a T-shirt that clashed horribly with his red hair.

He pulled up short and eyed me with a none-too-happy expression. "Nathan's been worrying himself sick over you. Get your backside upstairs and set his mind at ease that you haven't done anything stupid."

"Sorry," I mumbled as he pushed past me.

"Bailey, I like you a lot, you're a great guy, but you need to pull your head out of your arse because you'll never find the sun up there." With that, he patted me on the arm and rushed off down the street.

I didn't bother to answer because, what could I say? I did have my head stuck up where the sun didn't shine. I just needed to find the right crowbar to prise the fucker out. I grumbled to myself as I walked up the stairs with my feet dragging. Not at all sure what kind of reception I was going to get from Nathan, I used the stairs to delay the inevitable.

On the second floor, I went to Nathan's office to check to see if he was there. Finding it empty, I went up the last couple of flights to the third floor where his apartment was. Sweating like a stuffed pig, I pressed the bell and held my breath.

The door opened without preamble and Nathan stood there, his expression unreadable as he eyed me from head to toe. "You've managed to crawl out from whatever rock you've been hiding under I see," he snarled.

My heart sank at the anger in his voice and I all but deflated in front of him. My shoulders hunched as I dropped my gaze to the floor and kicked at the ground absently, noticing I was still wearing Isaac's clothes.

"What have you got to say for yourself, Sarge? I've been fucking worried sick. You could have at least answered a text to say you were okay," he ranted as he stepped aside, opening the door to allow me past.

The air whistled through my teeth that he'd not told me to fuck off and shut the door in my face. There was no excuse for not responding to his texts.

"I'm sorry, Nathan." It was the truth, I was. I walked into the apartment and groaned at the delightful smell of home baking.

"Don't be getting any ideas about receiving treats. A naughty sub gets a punishment, not a reward," Nathan stated, though without his initial heat.

I nodded, then walked to the sofa and took a seat facing the large window. The view was distracting as Nathan came and took the seat next to me. He twisted so he was facing me, and I knew the second he touched my arm that he'd forgiven me.

A tear rolled down my cheek, followed by another. They dripped onto the wooden floor as Nathan waited me out. It took several minutes before the tears stopped flowing enough that I could talk.

"I wish you'd given me a warning on Saturday. I wasn't prepared for seeing him. For the feelings, the shame, the fear, the love. They floored me, I just needed out. Needed a moment to breathe and figure out what the fuck I wanted to do." I looked at Nathan's contrite expression. "It's okay, I get what you were doing, but a heads-up might have helped. Anyway, I've spent the last two days at Isaac and Ferron's house—"

"The fuckers never let on," Nathan ground out.

"I asked them not to, so don't go blaming them. Ferron was being a good friend, and Isaac, well, he's wrapped so tightly around Ferron's little finger, I'm sure there's nothing he wouldn't do for him."

"You got that right."

"You're not much better with Lenny, you know that, right?" I added, feeling a sliver of humour surface at the discomfort on his face, until I remembered my own shitty situation.

"Yeah, that may be so, but look what I gained."

There was so much awe and love in his voice that I bled a little for the lack in my own life. I chewed on my thumbnail, an old habit I'd broken years ago, as I eyed Nathan. "I found Jake and Sam in Jake's playroom this morning when I got back to the house." I spoke so fast it sounded garbled to my own ears as the blood pounded in them, but Nathan nodded.

"Then what are you doing here?" His blond brows rose and disappeared under his fringe.

I got up and walked to the window, gripping the ledge as I stared unseeingly over the city, images of Sam popping through my mind. The exuberant joy he'd exhibited, now that I reflected on it, was what had thrown me off balance. *What about his leg?*

That thought increased the sorrow I felt for the pain he must have suffered and guilt quickly followed at how he'd kept such a life-changing thing from me. *You rejected him!*

Regardless of the fact I'd rejected him, it would seem a secret part of me had always seen him as mine. The moment it registered that he wasn't, that he'd moved on with his life and found someone else, it had fucked with my head. I was totally screwed, and I knew it. I didn't want to be a Dom, and I didn't want to challenge Jake. Far fucking from it. Yet, I'd done exactly that when my past expectations got in the way.

Releasing my tight grip of the little ledge, I turned and faced Nathan. "When I rejected Sam, as I told you, I thought it was for the best for both of us. It appears I'd secretly harboured this notion that no matter what, he'd always be mine. Faced with the reality that he'd moved on, well, it had me acting out of character. Or maybe I should say *in character* for the army sergeant." I sucked in a shaky breath. "I challenged Jake."

The last part came out as a whisper, as if I were scared to admit what I'd done aloud. Nathan's face lit with humour, but he didn't laugh, so that was something.

"How did that go down?" he asked, his lips twitching as he stroked his chin.

I quickly ran through what had happened, skipping the part where Sam had ripped open the old wounds that had never healed. "It ended with him asking 'who was the Dom'. At that point, I did what I always do when faced with a personal crisis and high-tailed it out of there." I rubbed my hands over my face and then through my hair before I walked back to the sofa on unsteady legs. I sank down, grateful to be sitting as Nathan spoke.

"You've fucked up big time my friend. I get why. You've spent your whole life living up to other people's expectations, to the determinant of your own. The thing is, can an old dog learn new tricks?"

"Less of the fucking old, I'm only five years older than you," I said without any heat as I sank back into the cushions, feeling flattened by reality.

"I'm not sure I can," I answered truthfully. "You understand there has always been a part of me that wants to submit, to let go. What you don't know is how hard I find it when I've found a Dom to meet my needs. It's rare that I've found the head space to really let go. It seems the other part, the part that is used to being in charge, is so ingrained that it just doesn't seem to want to let go."

Nathan sat forward, his eyes narrowing as he took hold of one of my hands and drawing my full attention. "Sarge, answer me this, who has the power in a Dom and sub exchange? Who keeps control throughout?" The quietly asked questions were like mini-explosions going off inside my mind.

"The...sub," I stuttered, while my tongue felt too big for my mouth.

His eyes lit in approval and my heart quivered in my chest. How had I lost sight of

26

that? *You've not allowed yourself to truly let go since you fell in love with Sam.*

I gripped Nathan's hand tightly as the reality of the thought shook me. It was quickly followed by a replay of what had happened today. Had I fucked things up again? Would Sam give me a second chance to prove myself worthy of him? Would Jake?

Chapter Two

Sam

For the last couple of weeks, it was as if we'd all gone to our respective corners to let the dust settle. Except for Jake, who'd had to travel up to Scotland due to a problem with some architectural issues that meant the builder needed him on site. He'd left the Monday night it had all kicked off and wasn't planning to return until this weekend.

Only, there was one small problem with that, my newfound libido. It was like Sleeping Beauty awoken from her slumber, and I'd been in a state of constant arousal ever since. Add in that Jake had been clear about the rules he'd laid down when we'd talked after Bailey had left. There was to be no touching my cock, with one exception, bathing.

I eyed the unremorseful fucker as I lay on my bed while it waved at me. I'd woken from yet another hot, steamy dream of me and the two men that had acquired all my attention when I wasn't at work.

When I'd agreed to Jake's demand, I'd been working on the old assumption that my cock wouldn't show much interest, like the past several months. *Yeah, how had that worked out for you?*

"You know I'm not allowed to touch," I pointed out to my cock huffily, not feeling in the least bit silly when my balls ached with the need to come.

I was hornier than a bitch in heat, and how much longer I could keep obeying Jake was anyone's guess. Yet, being a submissive at heart, I'd no wish to do something that would garner me a punishment, especially after seeing Jake's playroom. *He won't know if you touch.* I rolled my eyes heavenward. But I'd know, and I'm shit at keeping secrets!

Shutting my eyes, I willed my dick to deflate, but a picture of Jake and Bailey weaved its way into my mind, so that didn't work. The image had somehow glued itself to the inside of my eyelids so that every time I shut them, I could see it clear as bloody day. That really did not help when all I had was sex on the brain.

As if on cue, my mind latched onto Bailey's face and doubts started to creep back in about whether Jake could give me what I'd wanted for more years than I cared to admit—Bailey. It felt inconceivable after everything, but my hope had been reignited and it was hard to extinguish it.

Uncomfortable, I reached down to rub at my right knee, recalling the question that had come up after Bailey had gone. Why hadn't he mentioned my leg?

I'd been so wrapped up in the past, I'd all but forgotten about it. It was only after Jake had helped me to get dressed that it struck me that Bailey hadn't brought it up. Could it have been because of everything else that was going on? It didn't seem to me like he'd looked at me any differently.

What I had noted got my heart fluttering madly in my chest. Had the possessive jealousy when he'd faced off with Jake been real? If it was, where did that leave the threesome idea? I sighed forlornly.

It had been the first time Bailey had shown his feelings for me outside of the friendship we'd developed over the years. I'd initially not realised what he'd revealed, with the hurt he'd inflicted being front and centre. It took a whole day for the reality to sink past another rejection. But where had it left me? *No man's land, that's where!*

Jake hadn't quite seen it that way at all. He had seen Bailey's behaviour as him needing time to get his head on straight. He'd assured me Bailey would be back. My stomach clenched. Was Jake right? I lowered my gaze to my now flagging cock and sighed anew.

There'd been lots of moments over the last couple of weeks where I'd doubted Jake's conviction, based on what had happened in the past. Yet, the love I felt for Bailey wouldn't be pushed away so easily with Jake's positive attitude refuelling me.

Then there'd been the text messages from Bailey. Nothing major, just a 'hey, how are you doing' type thing, but nevertheless, they left me feeling like I was standing on a precipice looking down at the valley thousands of feet beneath me. *Please don't let love kick me in the arse again, please.* I sent up a silent prayer as I sat up.

I eyed the shadowy room, looking for the crutches I didn't often use as I could easily hop about on one leg. But with how busy the bar had been of late, and the interrupted sleep from the sexy dreams, I wasn't sure I'd not trip and land on my arse. A groan rumbled up my chest when I spied them on the other side of the room, nowhere near in reach.

Resigned, I edged off the bed and crawled to them. The feelings of humiliation I'd felt in the beginning at having to learn to crawl and get up from the floor one legged had long since dissipated. Doing it in front of men with much worse injuries than me had cured me of my pity party. The time I'd spent in the rehabilitation unit learning to gain back my independence had taught me a valuable lesson, there was always someone much worse off. So, I'd buttoned my lip and worked to regain the freedom that came from standing back up on my own. The side benefit had been that it helped me figure out how to move as a puppy.

A smile spread over my face at how easy I'd found letting go in front of Jake. His joyous laughter had helped, along with the arousal he'd sported. It might have all gone to hell in a hand cart after Bailey interrupted our fun, but right up until that point, I'd been in seventh heaven.

My cock twitched and I shut off my train of thought as I entered my small bathroom. I laid the crutches against the toilet, next to the small glass shower cubicle that I barely fitted in. When the water had warmed, I made quick work of having a shower, using what I had to do today to keep my thoughts from going back to sex.

Isaac had thankfully taken me under his wing and given me a heap of information to ease me into the manager's role. Having tended bar for a couple of years before joining the army, I'd no problem with that part. Some of the training I'd done in the army had helped with managing people. As Scott managed the waitstaff for the restaurant, that left me to manage the barmen and circulating waiters in the bar.

Initially, I wasn't quite sure how it would work, but Scott and I had formulated a rota between us, and he filled in for me on my days off and vice versa. Seb and Nathan had been pleased we'd seen the two roles as basically the same. It probably saved them money as well.

That, however, didn't seem to be an issue given the takings the bar and restaurant were generating. For me it was no surprise. Carl and Lenny were phenomenal chefs, so the food was amazing. I was told Seb was just as good, but so far, I'd not had the privilege of trying his food.

We were heading into summer and the restaurant was booked solid until October. The tables and booths in the bar were similar. Today was all about planning the rotas and doing stock take.

My eyes rolled to the ceiling as I dressed. Stock take wasn't so bad, what was a real pain in my rear were the Excel spreadsheets that went with it. They'd quickly become the bane of my life, but as Isaac pointed out, a necessary evil to keep track of everything.

Dressed and out the door, the heat made my shirt stick to my skin before I'd taken a dozen steps. My plan to walk to the tube station quickly changed and I flagged a passing cab, thoughts of being crammed like a sardine in a tin with other sweaty people swimming around my head.

The App on my phone buzzed, and I grinned as I opened the message. Since Jake had left, I'd been receiving messages daily.

Opentoeverything: *Have you been behaving yourself, Pup?*

My cock stirred to life in my trousers at the term Pup, and what he was really asking.

Playfulpuppy: *Behaving myself...now let me think...have I?*

Opentoeverything: *Oh, we're feeling playful today are we...*

Straight after the message, a picture appeared of Jake's hand looking as if it were about to deliver a slap.

I swallowed the groan and shifted on the seat. The air con in the cab did little to cool me off as I typed.

Playfulpuppy: *Sir...respectfully, if you keep this up I might accidentally...come!*

Opentoeverything: *There'll be nothing accidental about it...remember, I promised you a reward if you stick to my rules, Pup...*

This time I groaned and had to push down against my dick to attempt to stop the throbbing ache.

"We're 'ere mate," the cabbie stated in a terse voice as I met his gaze in the rear-view mirror.

I worked on acting like I'd not been fondling my cock and pulled out my wallet after asking how much I owed. Giving him a hefty tip, I exited the cab into a wall of sticky heat. Pocketing my phone and needing a few minutes to get my thoughts out of my pants, I walked into the underground carpark. My shirt clung to my back by the time I entered the bar while my trousers chafed the tops of my thighs.

"Fuck, it's hot out there and it's only the middle of bloody June!" I exclaimed to Scott and Isaac, who were stood at the bar as I walked towards them. The cool air in the bar was a welcome relief.

Isaac gave me a half-hearted smile. "Yeah it is."

"You all right, Isaac?" I glanced from him to Scott, my brows rising at his unhappy tone.

Scott gave me a pinched smile at my question and patted Isaac's arm. "Isaac's just heard that they've confirmed the date for Ferron and Lenny's case. The court case starts in two weeks."

Isaac sighed. "A part of me wants this to be over with. But with all the other shit Ferron's been through, I want him to have a little more breathing room." The wealth of emotion in his voice when he spoke about Ferron left me feeling a stab of envy.

Pushing it aside, I reminded myself what Ferron had been through and that he deserved to find happiness. It seemed some dude from Ferron's past had kidnapped him and Lenny at New Year and had beaten them both up before Lenny had brained the guy with a bottle of wine.

There'd subsequently been a couple of other issues, and Nathan had upped security in The Playroom, insisting Ferron stay behind the bar. At the regular managers meeting, Nathan had only given the barest of details about why they wanted Ferron to stay where someone could watch out for him. Ferron and I had become friends, and although he talked to me, he'd not mentioned what had happened, so I'd let it be. All I knew was that it was a totally fucked-up situation and the up-and-coming court case wasn't going to resolve everything.

"I'm not sure what to say. But it has to be positive that you've got a confirmed date, right? It also means that the not-so-secret trip to China can be planned, right?" I blushed as I recalled how Ferron had asked me to keep schtum about him talking to Nathan about planning a holiday as a surprise for Isaac. However, when Isaac asked where Ferron was and used his Dom voice, I'd confessed faster than the speed of light. It was so embarrassing.

A hint of a smile appeared on Isaac's face. "Yes, there is that. Anyway, let's crack on. We've got a lot to do today. I've created some new spreadsheets—"

"Oh dear God, save me now," I complained, making Scott laugh and breaking a little of the tension in the room.

"Give over, you know you love 'em," Isaac stated in a dramatic voice.

"I love them," I shuddered, "like I'd love a lobotomy."

Scott snorted as Isaac laughed. "Well, as a lobotomy is not on the agenda, we'll stick to spreadsheets."

"You know you're torturing me?" I quipped back as Isaac grabbed the file off the bar and walked to a booth to sit. I followed with Scott, and though I'd complained, I realised that I felt nothing but contentment as we started to go through the invoices first.

All I needed now was for my personal life to follow suit. Easy!

Chapter Three

*J*ake

The traffic was murder on the M71 as the lanes merged heading towards Glasgow. It was a relief when the signs for Carlisle appeared and I changed lanes to head back down south. The last three weeks had been hard going. There'd been a moment in the middle of the second week when, faced with yet another angry builder who thought my plans were shit, I'd wondered why the hell I'd thought architecture had been my dream.

I cricked my neck from side to side to ease a little of the tension in my shoulders. As my neck cracked, I groaned in pleasure. Swapping lanes, I moved over to the slow lane and put my BMW in cruise mode. I had at least eight to ten hours of driving in front of me, depending upon the traffic. A part of me wished I'd flown, but I'd needed some thinking time and driving always allowed me to do that.

After Sam had left my home three weeks earlier, I'd wandered around waiting for Bailey to return, feeling more certain than ever that I could be in a ménage à trois with these two men. Unfortunately, Bailey had not reappeared before I'd got an urgent call to go to Scotland, so I'd left him a letter after I'd packed.

Every day, I'd messaged him and Sam, and though Sam responded to my messages, Bailey had not. That was okay though because I'd contacted Nathan, having a feeling that was where Bailey would head after he'd walked out. I'd been right, and though Nathan hadn't said much about what they'd discussed, he'd told me not to give up on Bailey.

I chuckled at the idea. There was no way in hell I was giving up! I'd had three weeks to figure out how I could make it work between us. Excitement buzzed past my weariness and I recalled that Sam had the following day off. For my plan to work, I needed to talk to him and see if he was up for a change of address.

A churning started in my stomach at the importance of fitting the first piece of my plan into place. Close proximity, I felt, was the key to knocking Bailey's walls down. He'd put distance between him and Sam, it was time it was removed. My hands tightened on the steering wheel and I exhaled slowly. *I've got this!*

A nervous flutter followed, but I reminded myself this was how I always felt when I set my mind to something.

***

Ten hours later, my arse was numb and my lower back wondered why I'd tortured it by sitting for so long. I'd stopped at the services earlier to message Bailey and let him know when I'd be home. I just hoped he'd not run off.

I exited my car and took a moment to enjoy the evening sky that was a blaze of reds and oranges. Inhaling the familiar scent of London, I stretched and enjoyed being out of the car and at home.

Warm air brushed against my bare arms to remind me of the heat difference between London and Scotland. There, it had hardly crept above seventeen degrees. Here, it had to be at least ten degrees higher. I dropped my arms and acknowledged that the two pit-stops I'd allowed myself in my rush to get back were a distant memory. Thirsty and in need of a decent meal, I grabbed my suitcase and briefcase out of the boot with my mind full of having a glass of wine while I picked a takeout place to deliver some food.

After unlocking the door, I entered the house. Inhaling, I groaned and tilted my head, sniffing the heavenly scent of food! I dropped my bags to remove my shoes before picking them back up to head silently up the stairs. Was that curry I could smell? My stomach growled unhappily when I stopped on the second floor and took the time to drop off my bags before continuing up to the third floor.

The scent was forgotten as a flare of arousal tugged low at my gut, quickly followed by pleasure at finding Bailey home. Images of the future flooded my mind and my heart fluttered rapidly.

Don't get ahead of yourself.

Completely relaxed, Bailey hummed along to the music he had on low, seemingly lost in the simple task of cooking as I watched him unobserved. He stood on the far side of the room in front of the cooker. His back to me, he wore a pair of cut-offs that revealed his tanned, muscular legs and hugged his perfect arse. The T-shirt he wore was nondescript, yet my hands itched to touch the soft material that clung to his body like a second skin. His back rippled as he reached for something off the side. Then he stilled, his body tensing.

Seeing I'd lost the unguarded moment that revealed how very little Bailey let himself relax around me, I spoke. "Hey, you got enough there to share with a starving man?"

He slowly turned and his face revealed nothing as his gaze swept over my creased trousers and wrinkled shirt that I'd rolled up past my elbows hours earlier. "After your text, I added extra." His voice betrayed his nerves.

I kept the smile off my lips as he shifted back to face the cooker and picked up a spoon to stir one of the silver pots. Noticing how his fingers shook, my own nerves thrummed with anticipation. "You're a lifesaver. I thought I was going to have to order takeout." Deepening my voice, I walked to him and stopped a couple of inches from his back.

The masculine scent he liked to use tempted me closer. A visible shiver ran down his body and he seemed to stop breathing as I lifted onto the balls of my feet to look over his shoulder and down at the cooker. Warmth filled my chest as I took a deep inhale of what I thought might be my favourite curry. *He'd added extra my arse! He'd made this for me.*

My face barely a couple of inches from his, I turned to look at him. His eyes were glued to the pot he was stirring with intense concentration. I, however, could feel the waves of uncertainty pouring off him. "That wouldn't be my favourite curry, would it?" I dropped my voice another octave and whispered in his ear, "Did you do this to please me?"

He shuddered and his eyelids drooped. The hand stirring the pot stopped moving as if he'd lost the ability to recall what he was doing. His reaction was so perfect, I struggled to keep control of my own body. "Because if you did…" I trailed off and moved my lips to the rim of his ear and blew.

He pressed back against me as the sound of ragged breathing drowned out the soft background music. Temptation to reach around his hip and grip his cock to see how aroused he was, left me a little breathless.

The promise I'd made to Sam, that this would always be about the three of us and no one would be excluded, allowed me to ease back. Once I'd made that promise, I knew I'd never break it, regardless of how much I wanted to see Bailey submit to me right then.

I can't say I wasn't disappointed by Bailey's small moan of distress as he sagged against the counter. There was a strong urge to soothe him and give reassurance his efforts would be rewarded, but before that I needed a moment to clear the lust from my brain, so I went to the wine cooler. "Would you like a glass of red or white wine?" My hand hovered over the choices as I glanced back at Bailey. He'd gone back to staring at the pots.

"Yes, and red, please, if that works for you." The undercurrent and meaning behind his word choice left me grinning.

"Red it is." I took a bottle of Rioja and went to the cupboard to find two wine glasses.

After setting the glasses on the table, I went to grab cutlery to set the table. By the time I'd finished, Bailey was plating the food and warmth once again flooded my chest with the reality that he'd thought about the timing for my arrival home to coincide with his cooking dinner.

I'd never wanted a slave, but someone that was thoughtful to my needs? Yeah, I could get used to that. None of my previous subs had been particularly good in the kitchen, so I'd tended to make all the meals. *Bailey isn't your sub.*

He will be!

The man in question tugged me from my thoughts as he laid a plate of fragrant food in front of me. My mouth watered and my stomach snarled, recalling the dry sandwich I'd picked up at some services I'd stopped at hours earlier.

Only when he placed his own plate down did I reach out to touch his arm. He stiffened briefly before relaxing, and I gave him a big smile. "Thank you, Bailey. This looks delicious and I can't wait to get stuck in. Living off takeout and hotel grub can wear a bit thin after three weeks."

He gave a small nod and looked at the hand that remained on his bare arm. I gently caressed the warm, scented skin before removing it. His mouth opened, then as if he thought better of whatever he was going to say, it shut, and he took the seat opposite mine. I let it go and focused my attention on the meal he'd made. The curry was spicy, just how I liked it, and the rice was fluffy.

I'd nearly finished my meal before I looked up to see he was pushing his food around the plate. My brow rose and I swallowed my mouthful of food. "Aren't you hungry?"

His gaze remained fixed on his plate as he shrugged.

When that seemed to be the only answer I was going to get, I picked up the napkin I'd placed on the table and wiped at my mouth. I picked up my wine and took a sip, savouring the rich burst of flavour that took a little of the heat out of my mouth as I eyed Bailey over the rim of my glass.

Chapter Four

The second Jake sat back in his chair, my already nervous stomach knotted further. Any hopes of acting normal and eating flew right out the window at the weight of his stare on me.

There was something different about him. I'd not been able to pinpoint it until I'd got a good look at his face. Determination, it was there in the depths of his eyes and it made me uneasy and so fucking excited. In Dom mode, Jake was like catnip to a cat. My cock was rock hard, and I'd struggled to not get down on my knees and beg for a little more of the attention he'd given me while I'd been cooking.

I could still feel the warm traces of his breath against my skin. I'd been anxious he'd go further, then disappointed when he'd pulled back, leaving his sentence unfinished. Had he been about to promise me a reward?

The nerves were back, and I clutched at the fork I still held in a death grip. In the three weeks he'd been away, I'd had little else to occupy my mind but the letter he'd left on my bed.

Bailey,

Unfortunately, I have a work-related crisis in Scotland that requires my urgent attention, otherwise I'd have waited to speak with you in person.

I understand that your role in the army put you into a dominant position, but you are no longer in the army. That being said, I see beneath the veneer you use to cover what your soul craves, submission. Can you be honest and face what you want?

I hope so, because I feel three is the magic number when it comes to all of us. If you hold the same belief, then here's rule number one: No touching your cock.

While you think about the answer and my first rule, know this. Your actions today require a punishment. I will not tolerate you challenging me or inflicting hurt on Sam. I want you to think about this and know I'll be doing the same. There will be a worthy chastisement for your actions on my return, if you choose us.

I'm unsure how long I'll be gone, so use the time wisely.

J

Every time I'd read the letter, I'd felt a shiver of excitement. Could I have it all? Could I have the love of my life and a Dom? Where there had once been fear, now all I felt was a flare of optimism at the possibilities Jake offered.

On the back of the illuminating conversation with Nathan, where he'd relayed back to me what submission was all about, I'd worked to reset my mind, my thoughts. *I retain the power in submission. I am the one in charge.* It was my new mantra.

It was hard to acknowledge that I'd got lost in what was expected of me and had forgotten that simple principle. The knowledge had somehow liberated me, but also left a heavy weight of guilt hanging around my neck for yet again hurting Sam in my confused state. Jake's threat of a punishment was deserved so I'd felt no fear, only nervous excitement.

Was what he'd done in the kitchen part of the punishment?

"I can all but hear the wheels turning in your head. Ask me?" he said, his voice deepening.

I dropped the fork I'd been pretending to use to eat and glanced at Jake from under my eyelashes. "The letter...you mentioned a punishment..." The words dried up at the glint in Jake's eyes as he pinned me with a molten stare that seared my skin.

He carefully placed the glass he held down on the table. The clink of glass touching wood was drowned out by the whooshing in my ears from the blood rushing in my head. He leant towards me and rested his elbows on the table as his fingers clasped together and his chin came to rest on them. "I made a promise to Sam and I'll make the same to you now. So as not to exclude anyone, we will not use my playroom unless all three of us are present."

My lips thinned as an image of Jake and Sam sprung into my mind and I struggled not to point out what had happened before.

Jake's brow rose as his gaze searched my face, and I realised I'd given away what I was thinking. He waited a moment, giving me every opportunity to argue.

The nod of approval he gave me when I remained silent caused a glow of happiness to spread through me.

"That morning, I'd every intention of speaking to you both about the possibilities of a ménage à trois. I'll admit, when Sam gave his submission and trust to me, I got carried away—"

"What's to stop you doing that again?" I growled, forgetting myself as my temper bubbled over and joined the jealousy at what he'd got to share with Sam.

His mouth pinched into a thin line and his eyes darkened. "I'll ask you again...who is the Dom?" The whole room seemed to vibrate with excess energy as he waited for me to reply.

This is it, come on, let go. I prayed I was making the right decision as I dropped my gaze and answered in a breathless whisper, "You, Sir."

A sound of air hissing between teeth filled the silence that followed. It registered somewhere in the back of my mind that the CD I'd put on had stopped playing. My chest burned as I waited for him to say something, anything.

I felt the shift of air before a hand touched my cheek to encourage me to look up. The tight band released the second I saw the pleasure and arousal on his face.

His fingers stroked my cheek. "You don't know me well enough to know that I'll never break any promise I make. And trust me, right now I want to show you how much I want to break it and have you over my spanking bench to cane your arse until you can't sit down," he rasped, then sucked in several breaths as it looked like he struggled to retain control of his emotions. "I want this to work between us. I'll always put both yours and Sam's needs first, that I can promise." He traced my lips before his hand dropped away, much to my disappointment

He moved to take his seat and lifted his glass. There was a slight tremor in the fingers holding the stem as he took several sips of wine, his gaze again fixed on mine. "Sam has a day off tomorrow, and I've invited him to come over for the day. I want the three of us to spend time together so we can talk about expectations, needs, and limits. It's important to communicate openly when starting a new relationship. It will undoubtedly be harder to navigate with there being three of us. I'll only tolerate honesty, Bailey. There will be no hiding, is that understood?"

The deep timbre of his voice, along with the aura of dominance that had increased as he'd spoken, left me dry mouthed. Understanding a nod would not work right then, I picked up my own wine and gulped it down, letting the buzz take the edge off my nervousness.

He remained watchful but said nothing more as I emptied the glass. I lowered my gaze after placing the glass down and got off my seat. His pose remained relaxed, however there was a tension radiating off him that said he was anything but.

I hesitated for a moment and pleaded silently that I wasn't about to make a fool of myself as I lowered into a pose of submission at the side of his chair. My backside rested on my heels as I rested my palms on my thighs and lowered my head. The seconds stretched for what felt like forever before he moved, and his hand stroked over my hair in a gentle caress.

"You honour me, Bailey, with your submission. I'll treasure the gift you've given me." His voice was thick with emotion and a tear slid heedlessly down my cheek.

His finger followed its path as he wiped it away. "Know this, you're beautiful as you kneel for me. It makes me ache for you." His hand lingered another moment before he removed it. My skin tingled from his warm touch, even as my heart beat faster from his confession.

I swallowed the urge to beg for more and willed the night away and Sam's arrival closer. Would Sam accept me like this?

You'll find out in the morning!

The pleasure turned to dread.

Please, God, let Sam accept who I really am.

Chapter Five

Sam

I'd been so nervous, I had to change my T-shirt because of the sweat patches that had developed under my arms. I sniffed my armpits before shrugging into the fresh T-shirt. Rolling my eyes heavenward at the pointless shower I'd taken, I groaned at how I'd been dithering for the last hour over the stuff I'd packed in the overnight bag Jake had suggested I bring with me.

Leave now before you change your mind!

Picking up the bag, and the additional one containing my puppy gear, I eyed the crutches laid by the side of my bed. Should I bring them too?

The second guessing myself had started when Jake had messaged me last night to advise that Bailey was spending the day with us. That right there had sent me into a tizzy, and I'd hardly slept a wink.

There'd been no mention about what that was going to entail, but when Jake had insisted I bring some things so I could stay overnight, my mind had taken to jumping around all over the place like a child on a trampoline. I had no clue where my thoughts would land next, hence the need to swap out my T-shirt for a fresh one.

Taking a deep breath, and then another, I willed myself to calm the fuck down as my eyes returned to my crutches.

Did I want to look like a dick hoping about on one leg? Nope, I did not. Would the crutches just make my disability stand out more?

"Dear Christ, get a fucking grip. Take the crutches and if Bailey flakes on you again, you'll have the answer." It took a second to realise I was talking aloud, and I shook my head.

"Bloody typical, I'm losing my mind right when I need it!" I complained as I reached for the crutches and righted myself carefully.

Out on the street, I waited for Jake to collect me. The wall of sticky heat left me eyeing the jeans I'd put on in lieu of a pair of shorts with disdain. I didn't have long to think about going back inside and changing before Jake's crystal-grey BMW pulled up. There were several horn blasts as he double-parked right next to where I was standing. I chuckled as he paid them no mind and got out of the car.

In my hurry to not keep him waiting, my foot caught on the uneven pavement and I lurched forward. With my hands full, I braced to fall on my face, only to find myself caught in

Jake's arms. The fragrant scent of his aftershave surrounded me while the warmth of his body pressed against mine and awakened the need that was never far from the surface these days.

I groaned and heat flooded my face when his brow rose as he stared into my eyes. Then he got a devilish glint in his eyes that arrested the breath in my lungs. He shifted my body easily so that I was pressed more firmly against him while he whispered in my ear, "I think someone is excited to see me."

God I was panting. Could this be any more embarrassing?

"It would only make a liar out of me if I said no. Not when my cock is about to burst out of my jeans and greet you with an eagerness that would embarrass anyone who cared to look. I think it might be safer if you let me go." I finished on a strangled moan when his eyes darkened with desire at my honesty.

"I've never been one to play things safe...but I'll let you go for now."

Oh buggering-hell!

This sexy side of Jake was far to fucking temping when I'd had nothing but filthy dreams to fuel me in days, weeks. I didn't get a chance to say anything about that as he took my bags and crutches from my sweaty hands.

"I'll put these in the boot while you get in the car, Pup."

There it was again, *'Pup'*. Fuck, it melted my insides faster than butter in a microwave. I wanted to spread myself all over him when he called me that. Panting like the pup I wanted to be for him, I got into the front seat and buckled up.

Once he was back in the car, I noticed he'd dressed for the weather. His stylish shorts in dark-grey matched the paler-coloured, V-neck T-shirt he wore. On his feet he wore a pair of classic boat shoes in black.

I looked at my scruffy jeans and the creased T-shirt I'd pulled out of the dryer, and not bothered to fold, and sighed. To distract myself, I looked out the window at the passing traffic, feeling more than a little intimidated by how put together he was.

His hand touched my thigh, and I took a second to compose my face before I offered him a smile I wasn't quite feeling.

"What is it? That sigh sounded ominous. Have you changed your mind?"

Strain appeared around his mouth and eyes as he stared at me for a brief second before looking back out the window at the road.

"Look at you."

His brow wrinkled as he did as I asked. He glanced back at me with confusion on his face. His gaze moved back to the road and the furrows on his brow deepened.

"You're all put together, and well, look at me."

His face morphed into a smile that hit me right in the heart, its aim deadly. "I was looking at you. I see you. I see a man who I'm excited to spend time with. I see a beautiful man full of honour and integrity—"

I held up my hand to stop him, but he was watching the road so I spoke over him. "You're...making...me blush, man," I stuttered.

"Truth is important to me. All I'm doing is telling you what I see, Pup."

Emotions I wasn't anywhere near ready to face surged up, but I was spared from saying something I might regret when a horn blared and Jake cussed, switching lanes. I released a breath then quickly inhaled, willing my heart to behave itself as Jake concentrated on the busy traffic.

The silence between us wasn't uncomfortable, and I relaxed against the seat and shut my eyes. It felt like seconds before the car stopped in Jake's parking space and I realised I must have dozed off.

I gave him a sleepy smile as he shifted his body towards me. His face wore a serious expression as he reached out to take one of my hands, and my heart flip flopped in my chest.

"I know we've talked about what is about to happen today, but if at any point you don't feel comfortable, I want to be assured you'll use your safe word so we can stop and you can explain what's wrong," he stated, his gaze scrutinizing my face.

The one thing I was starting to love about Jake was his directness. "I'm not going to say I'm not nervous about what happens when I walk into your home. That I'm not scared about how Bailey will see me *now*!" I sucked in a choppy breath as I met Jake's direct stare, dropping all my barriers. "I want this, not just Bailey, but you too. I'm not sure if it's just lust I'm feeling with the images you've been cruel enough to paint in my head, but I'm willing to go with it."

His devilish grin was back, and his fingers stroked over my skin, leaving small fires in their wake. "Is it wrong to want my pup to be able to visualise what it might be like between the three of us?" His laughter was wicked as he squeezed my fingers.

A shiver skittered down my spine while my dick bucked with excitement. "Visualise? Fuck, you've all but painted pictures under my eyelids in indelible ink!"

His laughter filled the car as he dropped my hand to exit the car. "That's right, laugh at me," I muttered

He didn't halt as he went to the rear of the car, but I heard him say, "I'm laughing with you, Pup."

I didn't argue because really it was a little funny if I ignored the boner I was sporting and that it was me he'd been tormenting.

I exited the car, freezing as the door to the house opened to reveal Bailey. His face was a mask of indecision as he fidgeted but remained where he stood. My heart swelled with the love that had never died, no matter how hard I'd tried to squish it. The love worked to mask the hurt he'd inflicted, even when my head went over our last meeting. I'd been brutal about how we'd left things. Would we be able to work through the hurt and pain?

Doubts crept in the longer Bailey remained staring at me.

I was distracted by Jake coming around the front of the car with my bags and crutches. It was then that Bailey walked down the path and wordlessly took my crutches in one hand and held out the other to me. The breath I'd not realised I held whooshed out so fast, a wave of dizziness swept over me. I blinked rapidly, looking between Jake and Bailey as I swallowed hard and took a firm grip of his hand. The warmth of his skin touching mine felt electric. The years of craving the smallest of touches from this man all landed on me at once.

The two men flanked me, and I couldn't pull a thought together with how overwhelming it was to be between them. A blush of heat rode to the surface of my face. I shut my eyes when I registered how aroused I was. Somehow, the images I'd been creating were nothing compared to the reality, and we weren't even fucking naked!

A gentle touch to my arm from the side Jake was stood on was enough to get me to open my eyes and look at him. "I'm feeling a little overwhelmed right now," I said to the brow he lifted in question.

"That's okay. I think we're all probably feeling a little like that right now." His hand remained on my arm as he glanced past me to Bailey. "How are you doing, Bailey?"

"I'm...scared," Bailey stuttered.

I tightened my hold on his hand and slowly moved to face him. The moment my back was to Jake, he pressed closer to me. His citrus scent calmed the madness in my chest as I started up at Bailey. "Is this what you want? Do you really want me as well as Jake?"

His fingers clasped mine painfully, and I sucked in a sharp breath, keeping my complaint to myself as he stared at me with deep sadness. The fact we were stood out on the street seemingly passed us by.

"I hurt you. I'm so, so sorry. I was a chicken, but more than that, I took away your choice to decide what was best for you. I wasn't honest about who I was deep inside, about what I need. I didn't face up to my feelings because it hurt me to think I couldn't have you, give you what you want and need. Will you give me a second chance to show that I'm worthy of your love?"

He sucked in a tremulous breath and took the step that separated us. The hand holding the crutches moved to the side as he held them out of the way. His other hand continued to hold mine as he lowered his mouth to within an inch of mine.

My chest billowed as I struggled to hold still, to think past the pain etched into his face. Then all rationality fled when Bailey's scent combined with Jake's and surrounded me.

Hot, I was so hot.

I was unsure if it was the heat of the sun blazing down on me, or Jake's presence at my back and Bailey's at the front of me, but sweat gathered on my upper lip. The seconds crept by as Bailey stood there, his breath touching my lips as it puffed past his open lips. His eyes searched my face, and it suddenly dawned that I'd not replied.

I licked my dry lips and tasted the salt of my own sweat. The buzzing in my ears increased as I reached up to cup his cheek with my free hand, leading with what my heart wanted. The brush of his whiskers tickling my palm affirmed that this was real, that I was indeed touching Bailey. I sighed in pleasure and let my fingertips trace over his face.

Jake's chest pressed firmly against my back, and he groaned while Bailey remained utterly still, his eyes wide and uncertain. I'd had weeks to think about the whys behind Bailey's behaviour and it hurt, I couldn't deny it, but I also understood it had been hard for him. That made it easier to confess to my feelings.

"I love you." The lightness that came from saying the words felt perfect in the moment where I pushed aside my own hurt to give Bailey the piece of my heart he'd owned for years.

His large body shuddered, then his hot breath merged with mine as our lips finally touched. I'd dreamed so often about how it would feel, yet the reality was beyond my wildest expectations. The gentle glide of his lips as his tongue slid over mine in a breath-taking duel of sensuality, left me melting back against Jake while Bailey pressed closer to me, trapping me between both men.

Chapter Six

*J*ake

Watching what was unfolding in front of me was too much to bear, so I dropped the bags I was holding, needing to be a part of what was happening. I pressed firmly against Sam and he vibrated against me, mewling into Bailey's mouth. My arms moved around Sam until I could touch Bailey. The second I slid my hands up his back, he made a rumbling noise that was quickly followed by Sam grinding back against me.

The kiss went on and on for what felt like hours, and it was glorious to watch. Bailey was gentle and reverent as he kissed Sam for the first time. It stole my breath and removed any doubt I had that this might not work between the three of us, with Bailey and Sam having an already established love connection. I didn't feel excluded, far from it.

This moment was theirs, yet I'd been allowed to share it with them and that heightened my desire for both men. It was as if they were sharing with me their feelings for each other; as Sam trusted me to hold him while Bailey trembled at each stroke of my hands against his back.

Sam pulled back his upper chest, moving against mine. "Fuck, you're good at that," he gasped.

Bailey's hungry gaze met mine and his eyed begged for what he wanted. "Do you want me to kiss you, Bai? Do you want to taste me on your lips? Let me taste Sam on your tongue?"

Bailey's body rippled under my hands. "Please...Sir?"

I was sure Sam could feel my heart take flight at Bailey's answer, but he didn't say a word as his head twisted to look at me. The hunger in his gaze as he licked at his lips, as if tasting Bailey, made me yearn to kiss both men at once.

The sounds of the street infiltrated past my desire and I reluctantly took a step back. "We need to take this inside, *now*."

Neither man argued, but both released a noisy huff. My lips pinched together to stop a chuckle as Bailey threw a frustrated look at my mouth before he guided Sam into the house. Bending to pick up the bags, I hurried after both men.

Talking, we need to talk first!

I repeated it as I mounted the stairs, but no matter how many times I reiterated it as I walked up behind my men, I knew that if I let either of them near me right then, there'd be no talking.

As a Dom, I'd trained for years to ensure that I maintained control, so my sub was my sole focus. It was a reality check that these two men could snatch it away so easily. All I'd need now was for them to realise it and I'd be totally screwed.

Like you aren't already, look at them!

Look I did. They stood in front of the windows, the sun glinting off the glass, making them both glow in the light. One tall and broad, with years etched into his face, while the other was long and lean, his face full of optimism. They were polar-opposites, yet equally as alluring, equally as compelling. And they both called to my lonely heart.

Had I found the answer to my own needs in these two men?

The sense of rightness that accompanied that question said yes, so I trusted it, and dropped the bags onto the sofa as I came fully into the room. Neither man moved as they stared expectantly at me. Within two feet of them, I came to a standstill, my gaze switching between them.

Inhaling a deep breath to centre myself, I released it slowly. "I want to talk about what this means to the three of us, but the sexual tension in this room says you might find it a little difficult to concentrate."

Both men's faces heated, and Sam's right hand twitched at his side.

"What I'm going to do is propose we move the talking aspect to the playroom so that I can ensure you're both focused solely on me," I rasped in a deep, husky voice.

Their joint groans were the exact response I was after.

"Yes, Sir," Bailey muttered.

Whereas Sam answered excitedly, "Hell yeah."

I turned around and grabbed the bag Sam had brought his puppy gear in previously, heading down to the playroom, my palms sweating. I didn't need to check if they'd followed me, I could hear their feet on the stairs behind me.

Once in the playroom, I dropped the bag on the floor next to the chair. The room remained the same as I'd left it three weeks earlier, but much had changed since then.

I eyed the St. Andrew's Cross before looking at both men, holding hands just inside the doorway. I took a deep breath, and another, finding the centre I needed to keep control.

"I've spoken to you both independently about what I want to happen between the three of us"—as I spoke I walked over to them, holding their gazes—"and now I want to talk to you together. Communication is vital in any relationship. This, as I've said to you both, will be harder, being as there are three of us. But

I'm sure that if we are all *open* and *honest* then we can make this work."

I lifted my hands and cupped first Bailey's and then Sam's cheek, connecting the three of us as I continued to hold their gazes. The tension in the room buzzed against my skin and I embraced it, knowing what the rewards could be if this worked out between us all.

I continued to reiterate the promises I'd made to both men, that no one would play without the other being present. That the playroom was about the three of us and that it was important to me that it stayed that way. Bailey visibly relaxed and Sam didn't contradict me.

"Bailey, can you tell me what your preference is for submission?" The question seemed to throw him as his brows met in the centre of his forehead and he looked a little lost. "Do you live the life of a sub twenty-four-seven or is it just when you're doing a scene?"

He released a shuddery breath and went to look at Sam. "No, Bai, look at me," I growled before he could twist his face towards Sam.

His gaze lowered. "Sorry, Sir. I...I've never been allowed to live the lifestyle full-time, though I'll admit, I've thought about it...a lot."

I stroked his cheek, seeing how hard it had been for him to confess to his needs. "My previous relationships have been with subs that prefer to live the lifestyle full-time. It's what I prefer."

Sam's expression showed concern as he fidgeted before his lashes dropped to hide what he was feeling.

"Eyes on me, Pup. Remember, we need honesty," I chastised gently as I met his stare, and colour bloomed up his neck.

He shrugged. "Sorry, but I'm not sure I want to be a puppy all the time."

The seriousness with which he spoke released a little of the tension that had gathered in my shoulders. "That's perfectly acceptable, Sam. Being a puppy offers you a freedom to let go and release everyday worries, am I right?"

"Yeah. I love how the world can disappear while I play with my master. There's nothing more freeing." His face held an earnest expression as he looked to Bailey and gave him a smile. "I always had this urge to curl up on your lap and get you to pet me."

Slashes of deep red spread over Bailey's cheeks as his eyes hooded, and if I wasn't mistaken by the bulge in the front of his shorts, his cock thickened.

"You like that idea don't you, Bai? Pup curled up in your lap and him letting you pet him." My voice dropped and deepened as I painted a picture for Bailey. "Would you stroke down his naked back and over his tail to tease him?"

Sam groaned, his hand going straight for his cock. "No, Pup."

"You need to fucking stop, or I'm gonna come in my pants," he gasped, while struggling to do as he was told.

His whole body trembled as I stroked his cheek and gave him a wicked grin. "Do you think I could make you come, Pup, without touching you?"

"Oh crapola. You're killin' me, man" he complained in a strangled voice.

"Do you have a special tail you like, Pup? One Bailey could play with that moves inside you and rubs you in the right way. Look at Bai, look at how aroused he is thinking about doing exactly that."

Sam's pupils looked as if he'd been drugged as he did as I bid. His whole body juddered, and his hands fisted at his sides as he looked at Bailey.

Bailey wasn't much better as he met Sam's lusty stare. The tension between them was electric.

"Would you be gentle with your strokes, Bai, or would you be firm? Would you let your pup lick you, use your body as a chew toy?"

My chest heaved, watching as both men groaned and moaned. Their need was palpable as they struggled to obey me and not move. It was so fucking heady I wasn't sure I wouldn't come in my own pants right then, with the air ripe and thick with sexual tension.

"Do you like a chew toy, Pup? I could chain Bailey to the St. Andrew's Cross and let you lick him and use him as one big chew toy. Would you like—"

"Fuck...shit...ohhhhhh," Sam cried, his hips moving uncontrollably as the front of his light-blue jeans darkened. A fine sheen of sweat covered his face while his chest sawed as he worked to keep standing. Sam's cries turned into breathless moans as he lurched forward, and Bailey, quicker than me, caught him.

The second Sam was wrapped in Bailey's arms, he groaned and buried his face in Sam's hair, his body quivering repeatedly.

My eyes widened and I masked my chuckle with a cough. Had Bailey found his release as well? I eyed both men. "Did I give either of you permission to come?"

The utter stillness of both men made the moment precious before two sets of eyes glanced at me. One looked decidedly more contrite than the other.

"It's your fault," Sam accused. "You've been teasing me for weeks. And the no touching rule, well I didn't touch, did I?"

I laughed as I found no fault with his logic. I glanced at Bailey and tilted my head.

He lowered his gaze, but not before I saw the flicker of excitement at the possibility of a punishment. "Sorry, Sir."

Chapter Seven

Bailey

As I strolled down the busy street, the brush of my underwear against my arse reminded me of the day before. The heat of the day couldn't compete with the after-effects of what Jake had done to me. He'd shown me who was in charge, and it clearly was not me. His idea of a punishment for coming without permission left me with a mixture of emotions. While he'd talked through my hard and soft limits while tethering me to the St. Andrew's Cross, I'd stupidly thought Jake, being that much younger, might not be able to take me to the place I yearned for...subspace.

How did that work out for you?

The burn I could still feel over my buttocks increased with a flood of arousal as my mind went to the moment Jake made me see the error of my ways.

"Strip, Bai, now."

The growled demand left no room for arguing so I released a grinning Sam and did as I was told. The sticky mess at my groin revealed how much I'd enjoyed the visual Jake had painted for Sam and me. By the time I was fully naked, Sam had taken the one seat in the room. His was gaze trained on my naked body, excitement clear in his bright blue eyes. He didn't appear to have an issue with his sticky, cum-filled pants.

"What are your safe words, Bai?" asked Jake as he came and stood in front of me, his gaze no less excited than Sam's as it roamed over my body. My spent cock twitched and drew Jake's gaze, his lips forming into a killer smile that worked like a magic caress. I swallowed my groan as my cock plumped further and Jake's hand stroked down my flank. The warmth of his fingers set little sparks igniting under my skin, leaving a trail of fire in its wake.

His fingers squeezed a little harder and I gazed at him from under my eyelashes. "Safe words, Bai, what are they?"

A flush of heat rode up my neck as it registered what I was about to reveal. "I use...Sammy for 'I'm okay'. Sky Blue for 'slow down' and...October for 'stop'."

Sam became utterly still, and I struggled to not give him my full attention as Jake's eyes narrowed on me before he looked over at Sam.

"I was going to suggest you might want to change first...but I think we'll leave it for now." Jake's eyes twinkled with mischief as he glanced back at me. "Let's get you tethered."

Without preamble, Jake, who'd already moved the St. Andrew's Cross into the centre of the room, strapped my ankles and then my arms to the wooden cross. The coolness of the wood against my chest, and the feel of leather around my wrists and ankles was something I'd missed. I relished the feeling of handing over control to Jake.

Jake had me facing Sam so he could see how aroused I was becoming, my cock visible as it jutted forward.

Warmth spread up my back as Jake stroked from my neck and down my spine to the top of my buttocks. "You are not allowed to come until I give you permission, is that understood...sub?"

I shivered as the word sub was whispered into my ear.

When I didn't answer immediately, he took hold of my hip in a painful grip, forcing me to gasp, "Yes...Sir."

"Good, sub. You mentioned you prefer the burn to sharp pain, so I'll just use a flogger to warm your skin. Then we'll see if you can cope with more." The confidence in his tone was arousing, but I'd never reach subspace with only a flogger.

I barely had a chance to keep the thought in my head when Jake demanded, "You are to keep your gaze locked on Sam at all times. Sam, you are to tell me if he doesn't."

Bloody hell!

Sam shifted to the edge of the seat, excitement pouring off him. "I'm happy to help."

I swallowed hard and prayed that I wasn't going to be begging for mercy too soon.

A hushed silence fell in the room, the air of expectation growing between the three of us. I couldn't see Jake, but I could feel the weight of his presence against my naked flesh the same way I felt Sam's gaze on me. Exhaling, I didn't get a chance to take a breath when the strands of leather touched my left calf. Warmth flared under the skin as Jake stroked his way up my leg to the underside of my buttock.

"This flogger is one of my favourites. Do you know why?" he rasped as he swapped to my right leg.

"No...Sir." I gulped as hot licks of pleasure spread from my burning left leg to my groin.

"I had it specially made. The flanges, if used with a little force, will increase the intensity. It means, my beautiful sub, that you'll feel me for long hours after I've finished. Imagine how you'll burn for me."

I cried out as he moved from my right leg to my buttocks, his strokes landing in a maddening rhythm. Sam's gaze was feverish as he watched me writhe against the wood, my cock painfully aroused and dripping.

The burn merged with the pleasure and clouded my mind as I struggled to stay present. I wasn't sure how long he used the flogger to bring the blood to the surface of my arse as I mindlessly mewled and begged him to stop. My safe word never passed my lips.

I sagged against the now damp wood when it ceased. Sweat slid down the sides of my face as Jake appeared in front of me. His dark hair was sweaty, and his face was sheened with moisture. But it was the gleam of pleasure in his eyes I couldn't look away from as he asked, "Safe word?"

"Sammy, Sir." At my response, his nostrils flared. His gaze dropped to my cock and I shuddered at the dark intent I could see.

He shifted to the side and glanced at Sam. "Pup, can you see if I stand here?"

The air I'd just inhaled remained stuck somewhere between my throat and chest as I eyed Jake wearily. Was he going to flog my cock?

When he looked back at me, I had my answer. Christ!

I lost the ability to draw in breath at the first strike to the tip of my cock. The pain and heat were a mind-melding combination, and Jake didn't give me a chance to brace for the next strike.

"Motherfuckerrrrr!" I bellowed as Jake set up a pace that left me hanging in a place

between heaven and hell. The strands occasionally wrapped around my cock as my hips took on a mind of their own and thrust as far forward as possible so they could seek more.

The burning sensation down my back and legs increased as the flanges of the flogger warmed the painfully sensitive tip of my cock.

Nonsensical words poured out of my mouth as Jake controlled my body and allowed my brain to shut down. There wasn't so much a click inside me, more a sigh as the pain became a spider's web. The intricate threads covered the skin of my body in an immeasurable pleasure I'd never experienced before.

My gaze latched on to Sam's, the burning intensity, the love, were too much for my overloaded senses. Right then, Jake stroked the tip of my cock with a forceful hit. My mind spiralled out of control and everything became blurry as I cried out, "Please...oh god...help me...Sir!"

I hung suspended in the pleasure and the pain as my body lost control when Jake whispered in my ear, "Come for me, show Sam you're ours."

"Are you okay, man?" an unknown elderly voice asked, pulling me abruptly from my thoughts.

If I weren't already hotter than hell from where my head had gone, I would have been from the old guy's concerned stare. I hoped he'd not noticed the rather obvious bulge in my shorts that pulsed none too happily at the interruption.

How fucking embarrassing. Had I been about to come in the middle of the street in front of strangers from thoughts of what Jake had done to me? I shook my head in disgust when my cock throbbed against my zipper.

Trying to think about anything other than what was happening in my shorts, I gave the man, who had to be in his eighties, a forced smile. He eyed me like I might have lost my marbles. As I I glanced about, I could see why he might think that as I was in fact standing in the middle of the pavement, seemingly staring at nothing.

I gave a wry chuckle. "I'm fine. I've a lot on my mind." *Understatement of the year!*

"All right. I'd suggest in future, young man, you might want to sit in a café and do your thinking." He looked at the road only several steps away before he looked back at me. "It can be dangerous if you don't pay attention to what's around you."

Feeling like a small child who'd just been chastised by its elder, I nodded, "Yeah, I'll do that in the future."

There was an awkward moment before he left me and carried on down the street, heading the opposite direction to me. Some of the passers-by gave me an odd look as I stood willing my body back into some semblance of decency before I carried on to where I'd been headed, the Flamingo Bar.

Ten minutes later, I sighed in relief that I'd been able to keep my head together enough to reach the bar without any further incident. I exited the lift and immediately searched the room for Sam. The bar wasn't due to open for another hour, and I'd hoped to get a few minutes alone with him. My heart sank at only seeing Scott standing behind the bar. Hadn't Sam said he was working today?

Jake had a futon chair in his office that he'd moved into the playroom for Sam to spend the night on. A part of me had wanted to ask if we could all share a bed, but with everything that had happened in Jake's playroom, I'd felt a little out of balance.

A little out of balance, don't you mean more like a tightrope walker wobbling on a highwire over some huge drop!

I chewed my lower lip between my teeth as I gave Scott a nod of acknowledgment and he waved me over when I dithered. Yesterday, I'd had no time alone to talk with Sam and this morning he'd left before I'd woken up.

So where was he?

Chapter Eight

Sam

Coming out of the kitchen, I stopped dead in my tracks as I saw Bailey leaning against the bar. His cropped hair was a little longer than normal and the silver streaks were concealed more in the length. His dark eyes were fixed on Scott and he hadn't noticed me.

A wild fluttering started in the pit of my stomach as I acknowledged the fact Bailey had come to seek me out today, and the feelings that evoked. I'd left this morning, needing some time to regroup after the day before. What had happened in Jake's playroom had been exciting and left me feeling intoxicated, like I'd had one too many drinks.

Once we'd left the playroom, I'd gone to clean myself up. Those few minutes without lust clouding my mind, I'd chastised myself for doing what I always did when it came to my personal life, rushing in where fools dare to tread. It hadn't taken long to realise that when I'd declared my feelings to Bailey, he hadn't responded in kind. What did it all mean?

He kissed you like you've never been kissed before!

All right, but it's not the same as hearing someone tell you they love you!

Small steps!

I swallowed a sigh and moved slowly across the floor towards Bailey. My leg throbbed, reminding me that sleeping on a single futon wasn't the most comfortable thing to do. But when Jake's eyes had reiterated his promise to me that Bailey would be ours, I couldn't resist and I'd stayed. And if I were truthful, I'd not wanted to leave, especially when both men offered to cook for me.

We'd eaten together, and I noted there'd been no uncomfortable silences as we'd chatted about Jake's trip to Scotland. If anything, it had been a totally relaxing experience and one I wanted to repeat. Especially the after part where I got to sit in Jake's lap and sprawl over Bailey's legs. We'd vegged out in front of Jake's widescreen TV and watched the first film in the epic classic *Lord of the Rings.*

Bailey had been the one conundrum as his hand had roamed over my prosthetic leg, his face unreadable. Would he be repulsed when I was naked?

Recalling how perfect his body was and how I'd never be that again, old insecurities I'd tried to push aside, resurfaced.

"Oh, there you are, Sam," said Scott, causing Bailey to glance in my direction.

I schooled my features as I continued across the floor.

"Hey, Bailey."

"Hey yourself, have you got a couple of minutes?"

His eyes begged me to say yes.

"I've got a few things to do in the restaurant. I'll leave you to it. Good to see you, Bailey." Scott gave a wave, but not before he gave me an encouraging smile as he walked from behind the bar and headed off in the direction of the restaurant.

When he disappeared from sight, I met Bailey's gaze. "What's up?" There were nerves in my voice.

Bailey glanced at the nearest seats. "Can we sit?" He didn't wait for me to answer. He went straight to the booth opposite the bar, sliding in behind the round table to sit down.

I scratched at my chin as I followed and sat off to his left side. His gaze dropped to the gleaming wood in front of him as he traced a finger over the surface. The tension that hadn't been present the day before made an appearance as he remained silent.

Is he about to reject me again?

"Have you had second thoughts?" I rasped past my dry throat as my hand under the table rubbed at my leg.

His head shot up and he shook it violently. "Fuck, no!" He sucked in a breath, then another as his chest billowed. "I wanted to talk...to check you're all right with me crashing your party with Jake. Yesterday was pretty intense, and I worried that maybe you got carried away. That you might regret letting me be a part of what you'd started with Jake before I...came in the other week and interrupted you."

His face had lost some of its colour as he spoke, but I was too stressed trying to figure out if he was worried for me or himself. "Are you shitting me, man? I fucking told you I love you. I did that in front of Jake. Right out in the open for anyone to hear."

Air hissed out from between my teeth as I attempted to keep hold of old hurts. I ran my hands through my hair and stared at his crestfallen expression. "Why would I be having second thoughts? All along I've been honest about my feelings for you. The only thing I'm having second thoughts about is believing you might ever have feelings...for me."

His hand shook as he reached out towards me, his eyes sheened with tears as they stared into mine. "Years...I've loved you for years."

He released a tremulous sigh as I took the hand he offered, my heart leading the way as it always had with this man.

"I've fucked up. My whole life I've tried to live up to the expectations of others. I've known since I was a teenager my nature was submissive. Back then, I didn't stand a chance against my dad and grandfather when they started to smother me in their expectations. With my submissive nature and their demands, it was a foregone conclusion I'd do what they wanted. It formed some habits I've found hard to break."

His fingers tightened around mine, his other hand reaching into his pocket to pull out his phone. He laid it down and fiddled with the screen before he flipped it towards me. The picture must have been taken about five years before, judging by where I'd been at the time. I was standing with a man who had been killed in action not many months after Bailey could have snapped that picture.

An ache developed at the back of my eyes as I glanced back at Bailey.

"You see, it's possible I've loved you for longer." He sighed. "One sub recognises another, that was the first barrier. Then there was my job and rank. There was pressure from my family to climb higher up the ranks. Unfortunately, you then caught me on a really bad day when you came to talk to me. My dad had been taken into the hospital. He was gravely ill, and he was pushing me to accept the promotion I'd been offered."

My eyes widened, but I bit my tongue to stop myself from asking any questions, aware that he'd not finished.

"The added pressure from my Dad was not what I wanted, but with his life hanging in the balance, I was truly fucked at the time. I wanted you, your heart, the love." His eyes became distant as he stared unseeingly at me. "I was in shock—my father, then your declaration. At the time, all I could see was that I was unable to give you what you wanted, what you needed. Two submissives together, it would have been a recipe for disaster. So I hid behind a mask of indifference to shield you from future hurt"—a tear slid down his cheek as he focused on me—"while it broke my fucking heart. I swear to God, I thought I was doing what was best for you."

The anguished cry, full of hurt, as he finished matched my own. My chest heaved as I let go of his hand and shifted so that I could get closer to him. When Bailey noted the awkward way I moved, he slid around the seat until he was next to me. His hands cupped my face, his fingers wiping at the tears running unchecked down my cheeks. "I'm so sorry. Will you ever be able to forgive me?"

Oddly, after I'd spoken to him all those weeks ago about the hurt he'd inflicted to my heart, it felt like I'd taken the plaster off a festering wound and allowed all the crap to escape. Jake had surely helped with his unrestrained attraction, but he'd also helped me see past the old hurts to what could be, if I allowed it.

Could I fully trust Bailey to protect my heart and not break it again? Didn't I do that yesterday when I told him I loved him?

Remember, nothing is guaranteed in life! As if my leg wanted to remind me of that, a phantom pain shot through me. "Shit." I winced and fidgeted next to Bailey, his brow furrowing before his face fell.

"Okay...I understand—"

"It's my leg, man," I ground out as the pain intensified until I was breathlessly clinging to the table. The futon had clearly been a bad idea.

"What can I do to help? Do you need me to get you some pain pills or something?"

Some of my humour returned at his panicked expression as he eyed the leg pressed against his thigh. "Pain pills don't work on phantom pain," I said between a breathless laugh and cry.

His brows met in the middle a second before he reached out and started to massage the top of my thigh. The touch was firm but gentle as he worked to ease the knotted muscles beneath my trousers.

My pulse skipped several beats while I worked to figure out if Bailey touching my leg was what I wanted. Up to now, he'd not talked about my leg or what had happened, and I wasn't sure why.

His fingers worked to release a particularly hard knot just above my knee, and I tensed, undoing some of the good work he was doing.

"You need to relax, Sammy. Come on, breathe for me. Shut your eyes and work on focusing on what I'm doing."

His firm tone did silly things to me, while his use of my nickname took me straight back to Jake's playroom. The hand uncomfortably close to my cock and the vivid image of a naked Bailey strapped to the St. Andrew's Cross was too much. My eyes, that had started to drift shut, fired open as I exhaled on a breathy moan. Although I was in pain, my cock clearly hadn't got the message. Bailey's touch was doing more than easing the pain in my leg.

A flush of heat rode up my face when Bailey met my gaze with one brow raised. "Problem?"

"I'm gonna tell Jake on you." I said in a far too childish voice, seeing Bailey was aware of the effect he was having on me.

"Tell Jake what?" The man in question asked as he stood not more than three feet from us. Amusement sparked in the depth of his eyes when we both jerked to look in his direction.

I was the first to recover. "Bailey is teasing me."

"Thanks for that," Bailey muttered under his breath, before raising his voice as his gaze lowered. "I was trying to help ease the pain in his leg, Sir."

The battering my ribs took from my heart went unnoticed when Jake's eyes darkened, and his gaze swept my lap as he stepped closer to the booth to see past the table.

"Did you get our pup aroused, Bai?"

A shiver raced through Bailey as his fingers went lax against my leg. "Yes, Sir, I'm sorry, Sir. I was only trying to help him," he confessed in a breathy whisper.

The urge to pick up Bailey's hand and push it against my cock was hard to resist with Jake exuding his dominance over us both.

Chapter Nine

*J*ake

"**P**up, whatever you're considering doing, I'd think about it carefully if you don't want to find yourself in anymore hot water." I swallowed a chuckle when Sam visibly sagged against Bailey, his gaze moving briefly to his lap and Bailey's hand that remained on his thigh.

The bulge in Sam's trousers indicated how aroused he was. Bailey was not in a much better position, though he remained still, his gaze downcast.

When Bailey had said he needed to go out, I'd instinctively known he'd come to see Sam. Although we'd spent the day before, together, Bailey had been a little broody and I understood it might have had something to do with the past and Sam. I'd let him be yesterday, not pushing the issue after what had happened in my playroom. The vibrancy between the three of us during the scene had been breath-taking. When Bailey had finally let go, and accepted everything I'd given him, he'd been stunning. I was sure it gave him a lot to think about.

What I was unsure about was if Bailey had been aware that even as he'd come and entered subspace, he'd kept his gaze on Sam. It had been powerful and beyond anything I'd experienced with any other sub or boy I'd played with. The three of us had connected in a way that made it more important than ever to get what was happening between us right.

I'd acknowledged the tug of envy I'd felt at the love neither man hid in that moment of rapture. Yet I'd felt confident that it would work between us, and that hopefully, one day, I'd have the same connection with them as they had to each other. One thing I'd learnt as a Dom was patience. I had it in bucket loads.

"—it really is you two," Sam muttered.

I shook my head and tried to figure out what he'd been saying while I'd zoned out. "What is really us two?"

"You weren't listening." He huffed out a breath. "I was saying that I blame you two. I didn't have all these problems not touching my cock before." He rolled his eyes as his hands fidgeted on the table in front of him.

I saw Bailey's lips twitch, but the smile never appeared.

"As you're at work, I will have to wait to teach you what happens when you give me cheek."

His eyes widened, and he glanced sideways at Bailey as if looking for assistance. With Bailey's gaze downcast, I couldn't see his expression clearly, but the way he shifted marginally closer to Sam as if trying to reassure, showed his support.

"You were so good to help me with Bailey's punishment yesterday, I think it's only fair to let Bailey help with yours."

He froze, then his mouth opened as if he were about to argue, but Bailey nudged him in the ribs. I coughed to disguise my chuckle when Sam's mouth closed. Only when I felt in control did I carry on. "I came here today to talk to you *both* about a proposal." I stressed the word 'both', so Bailey understood I'd known this was where he'd been going when he'd left the house this morning.

He had the grace to blush, and his head tilted in silent acknowledgement.

Sam got a fevered look in his eyes. "A proposal?"

"Yes. How would you feel about moving into my home?" Thankful I'd not revealed the nerves I felt, I watched both men carefully to gauge their reactions.

Bailey sat up straighter, his chest appearing unmoving as we both waited for the silent man sat next to him, who looked poleaxed.

"What...really...the bed...my leg...seriously."

The jumbled words made little sense as I tried to figure out what he was meaning. "Yes, I really mean it. My bed is more than big enough to fit the three of us." I worked to keep my embarrassment under control when Sam's eyes twinkled with mirth. "I'm not sure what your worry is about your leg, unless it's the stairs?"

He shook his head. "Sorry, I wasn't making myself clear. My leg is sore after sleeping on the futon. When you suggested moving in, I couldn't see me doing the futon again."

Bailey released a noisy breath as I nodded and let the hope that was unfurling inside me have free reign. "No, the futon last night was just a temporary measure. I wanted to give you time to think about what happened between us all yesterday." My gaze moved to Bailey. "To think about what happens next. Bailey coming here today to talk to you was part of that, right?"

Sam wore a sheepish expression as Bailey nodded.

"Have you talked?"

"Yes…Bailey loves me." Sam's voice was thick with emotion as he looked from me to Bailey and back.

"I do." Bailey looked directly at Sam as he spoke and my heart rejoiced for them, even when it stung a little not to be included.

"So then, let's talk about what happens next." I kept my thoughts hidden as both men eyed me with mixed emotions.

Is it too soon?

That thought ran through my head a lot over the following days after Sam had said he needed some time to think about giving up his flat. We'd talked a little before Scott had returned and Sam had to go back to work. Bailey had been silent in the car journey home, going straight to his room.

He'd pretty much remained there, with the exception of coming to eat with me. He'd maintained his silence, and I wasn't sure if it was because of Sam needing time to think things through, or something else.

I'd let him be, hoping he'd come to me, but now I could see as we reached the end of day five, he wasn't going to talk to me willingly. I could hear him as I left my office to head up to have a shower. At least he wasn't hibernating in his room, so that was something.

On entering my bedroom, I pulled out my phone and messaged Sam.

Pup, you free to talk?

I'd been patient, but maybe it was time to mix things up a little. Ten seconds later, my phone rang, and I grinned at the screen. I swiped and put Sam on speaker, laying the phone on my bed as I started to strip.

"Pup, I've missed you," I said without preamble.

He chuckled. "You did?" He sounded happy at my confession.

"*I do*. You've been very quiet," I pointed out, not masking my disappointment.

There was a long drawn out sigh. "I... Do you think Bailey will still want me when he sees me naked?" he spoke in a rush, his insecurity clear to hear.

"Oh, Pup, is this why we've not heard from you? Bailey loves you." There was a hiccup sound as I continued. "Can I ask? Would you feel any differently about Bailey if the situation were reversed?"

I carried on unbuttoning my shirt, listening to Sam's breathing increase as he apparently took a moment to think about what I'd asked.

"No. No, it wouldn't make a difference to me."

"Then you have your answer. Bailey might have taken a little longer to find the courage to confess to his feelings, Sam, but I don't doubt his love is any less strong than yours. He strikes me as someone who loves with all his heart." My fingers trembled as I dropped the shirt onto the bed and stared down at the phone.

"I...want to move in. But do you think that maybe I should keep my flat for now and see how things work out? You might hate us all living with you."

I fist-pumped the air and caught my grinning face in the mirrored wardrobe doors. I looked like a crazy fool, but I didn't care. "I think that's perfectly acceptable. But know this, I won't expect you to pay rent here and pay for your flat too."

There was an indrawn breath as if he were going to argue.

"Am I your Dom?"

My question seemed to throw him as he exhaled down the phone in a noisy rush. "Yes…yes, but then what does that make Bailey?"

It was a clever move, because he'd neatly avoided answering me about the rent, but that was fine because I'd make sure to bring it up again later. "I think that's a question you need to ask Bailey, don't you?"

"Yeah, I suppose. But I thought if you were my Dom, that maybe you could ask him, or just tell me?" he wheedled in a voice that I struggled not to give in to.

"I am your Dom, and it's wonderful that you trust me in this way," I hedged for a moment, trying to find the right words while my heart swelled in my chest. "But by doing that, I'm excluding Bailey from the decision. You don't want to do that, do you?"

He gave a heartfelt sigh. "No, I don't…but for the record, I like the idea of you making decisions for me."

"I have no problem with that, Pup."

There was a small squeal of what sounded like delight before he started to talk ten to the dozen. "I'll pack my stuff. There isn't much. I'll need to sort a cab to collect me. That is unless you want to come get me. I'm finished for the day, so I could move in tonight. Will that work?"

I laughed at the barrage coming down the phone before I answered all his questions. A bubble of excitement fizzed in my chest that remained long after I'd ended the call, had my shower, and got dressed to go find Bailey.

The sound of banging pots led me up to the next floor as I rubbed my hands down my shorts. Please let this all work out!

Chapter Ten

*B*ailey

F uck, I'm suffocating!
Sweat beaded on my skin. How was it so
hot? I swallowed and tried to move, to
find a way of escaping from the wall of heat
that seemed to be surrounding me. My sleepy
brain tried to register what the problem was
when a hard dick poked into my left side. My
eyes slitted open.

Where was I?

Dim light cast shadows through the cream
blinds as my gaze roamed Jake's master
bedroom. *Jake's bedroom!*

I was in Jake's bed with Sam! It wasn't a
dream. As if to prove the point, Sam then
rolled his hips and made a little snuffling noise
as he tried to bury his head further into my
chest. I swallowed a chuckle, not wanting to
disturb either sleeping man as I looked over
Sam's shoulder to see Jake behind Sam,
spooning him. His arm was stretched over
Sam's hip and his hand lay on my stomach in
what felt like a show of possession.

Raw emotions left me blinking back the
sudden rush of tears clouding my vision. How
had I got so lucky?

When we'd left Sam earlier in the week, after he'd said he needed a little time to think about moving in with us, I'd been a grump. What didn't help was Jake. His dominating presence was so intoxicating to me that I'd taken to hiding out in my room.

Jake's promise to both me and Sam that we would work to build something together meant my sub side had to be tucked away, *again*. This had been far harder than it had been in the past. Living under the same roof as Jake, having experienced what he could offer me, was sheer torture. Sam added a new dimension, and I worried he wouldn't want to be with us full-time.

As I'd submitted to Jake, there was no way I wanted to go back to the way it had been before. The odd scene here and there when I had the time or the inclination to find a Dom. So I'd taken to spending as little time with Jake as possible while I'd waited, not so patiently, for Sam to make his mind up.

Then last night Jake had gone out, leaving my miserable arse behind, only to return with the best gift a man could want, Sam. With the bags they'd brought in from the car, I'd barely been able to stop myself crushing Sam to death in gratitude.

Sam snuffled again and pressed closer, making the heat level in my body go from hotter than hell to a volcano explosion. Sweat beaded at my hairline as I tried to disentangle myself from both men. This seemed to be a problem for Sam, and he clung on tighter, his arousal leaving a sticky trail on my thigh as he moved. Jake's fingers moved over my flesh, adding to my torment, and increasing my temperature by several more degrees.

I was actually panting like I was in the desert in sixty-degree heat. Yet the more they touched, the less inclined I seemed to be to make them stop. Especially when my cock took notice of what both men were doing to me. *Breathing space to cool down, who needed that?*

Last night we'd talked until the small hours of the morning. Jake had insisted we discuss what we all wanted from this relationship. It had been hard to put my needs into words in front of Sam, but I'd managed, just. Sam, as always, had been forthright about his wants. That he didn't see me as weak for wanting to be submissive to Jake, and on occasion to him, helped alleviate my doubts.

I gazed down at the man currently using my body as a pillow. Love swamped me and my lips formed into a smile.

Sam's mouth was slack, and his skin was flushed, incredibly long eyelashes fanned his cheek bones, and he had a bad case of bed hair, but he'd never looked lovelier. The dark circles that had been under his eyes when he'd arrived last night had faded and the strain around his mouth was gone.

When we'd finally headed to Jake's...*no, our bedroom*, Sam had hesitated when he'd started to undress. It was then, after Jake's prompting, he'd confessed to his worry about his amputation. I'd stripped, then gone to him, and with no prompting, I'd helped him undress. The arousal my body sported had shown him without words how wrong he was. The moment was made all the more special when Jake had come to help.

We'd kneeled before Sam as he'd sat on the bed and revealed his true vulnerability as I removed his prosthetic leg. I'd followed his instructions on what was needed to care for his warm stump. He'd been tense when I'd massaged the cream into the puckered flesh at the end of the stump, but I'd met his gaze as I stroked the scars, letting him know how brave I thought he was. Secretly, my heart had bled for how he'd had to go through life-changing surgery on his own, all because I'd rejected him. Hurt pinched my chest and my arousal flagged.

Almost as if Sam and Jake knew I was thinking about what happened, Jake's hand stroked at my chest while Sam's lower body ground firmly against mine and he moaned low in his throat. That had my body reacting immediately and emptied my mind of all thoughts. Another hip roll had Sam's slick cock glide up my thigh.

They're trying to kill me!

Convinced I was about to melt into the bed, I licked my lips and eyed Sam. His eyes gleamed in the morning light.

"You're playin' with fire," I growled.

"I was always good at avoiding getting burnt. Do your worst," he teased back in a sexy, sleep-roughened voice I could listen to all day.

A shiver of excitement was followed by a moan as Jake's hand roamed over to my nipple and pinched, hard.

"I think you might both be playing with fire, but that's all right, I have a hose that can help put out the fire."

Sam started to giggle. "You know that sounds real corny—"

"I'll give you corny," Jake rasped, his fingers continuing to play with my nipple. Then Sam's mouth formed an O shape as his hips shifted away, and I assumed, back against Jake.

"This isn't fair! I can't see what you're doing to Sam," I complained, then wished I hadn't when Jake's wicked laugh filled the bedroom.

"That's okay, pull the duvet down, Bailey and I will show you."

Sam groaned and I clenched my teeth together as Jake proceeded to twist my now throbbing nipple between his fingers when I didn't move quickly enough for his liking. Fully aroused, my cock rubbed against the cotton of the duvet as I pushed it down, then used my legs to kick it off. Once I had finally uncovered all of us, Jake released my aching nipple. The warm air against my sensitive dick did little to alleviate my growing need when both men's gazes travelled over my body. The possessive looks they both wore was enough to raise my temperature further.

"Bai, turn on your side to face Pup. Pup, open your thighs so I can slip my cock between your legs."

The sounds of heavy breathing filled the silence as Sam shifted, and I watched as he lifted his left leg to obey Jake's command. His eyelids dropped and his lips parted as he stared hungrily at me. I was sure I looked the same as him as I lowered my gaze to see the head of Jake's cock appear under Sam's balls.

Desire flooded my groin when, without being asked, Sam lowered his leg and clasped Jake's cock, leaving the leaking head exposed. My mouth watered for a taste of both men as Sam's cock jerked to show how much he was enjoying himself.

"Does my sub want to taste his Pup?"

"Oh god, please, Sir. I want to taste you too, please. Both of you," I begged, desperate for my first taste of both men.

Last night had been emotionally draining, so after we'd stripped Sam, Jake had encouraged us into the bed and had focused on us all getting used to being in the massive bed together. After Sam had confessed to how he wanted to be tucked in between us, Jake had ensured that happened. I'd drifted off to sleep painfully aroused but so fucking content when Sam had tucked himself against me.

Right now, I was anything but content, with my balls aching and my cock painfully hard. I wanted to taste my men. *My men*, fuck, that had a great ring to it.

"As Pup is owed a punishment, you can taste but you're not to make him come. Is—"

"What! How am I getting a punishment?" Sam blustered, his expression a little indignant.

I kept silent, seeing Jake's eyes darken and his aura of dominance increase, making the air crackle. Oh shit, Sam was in for it now. I almost felt sorry for him, but something told me he would enjoy whatever Jake had planned.

"Did you just interrupt me, Pup?"

The husky, rasped demand left Sam in no doubt that he was in trouble. Deep furrows appeared on his forehead and he wore a worried expression that Jake couldn't see.

"Erm…well…all right, I did, but…I was still half asleep," he stuttered to me, not looking back at Jake. It was as if he were trying to come up with a valid answer to stop Jake from doing whatever he was plotting. I met Jake's glinting eyes, my own widening. It was a good thing Sam couldn't see Jake's face right then. I swallowed hard, my body reacting to Jake's penetrating stare.

"Bai, I think Sam needs to be shown how a good sub is rewarded. Switch around, put your face down by Sam's groin and position yourself so your cock is next to Sam's face."

I didn't need to be asked twice and shifted quickly. The scent of pre-cum filled my nose as I inhaled excitedly. I gazed hungrily at Sam's aroused cock. It was around six inches, thick, and veiny. The head of Jake's cock protruded from under Sam's hairless sac. Pearls of pre-cum had formed in the slit and I wanted to push my tongue in for a taste.

The feel of hot breath touching my cock left me reeling with desire. I licked my drying lips and waited for Jake to tell me what he wanted me to do next.

"Pup, can you smell Bailey's pre-cum? See how aroused he is, knowing we're so close to his cock. Close enough to taste him."

Sounds of groaning nearly drowned Jake out as my body reacted to his words and the feel of puffs of air brushing against my leaking cock increased.

Chapter Eleven

Sam

For the life of me I couldn't get myself to shut my eyes and ears to block out what I could see and hear. Jake was fucking torturing me, and I fucking loved it...well, sort of. Bailey's cock was right there, so close. His scent was maddening. The beat of my heart left me struggling not to shake.

"Please, I'm sorry, I swear I am. I won't interrupt again, just let me taste Bailey," I pleaded. It was to no avail though. Jake reached out and took hold of Bailey's dick, moving until he was practically on top of me and able to lick the glistening head.

Bailey hissed loudly but my attention was on the man crowding me as he tasted what I wanted. A deep rumbled moan rose from the chest pressed against my back and Jake thrust his hips forward, his cock sliding between my clasped thighs. My thighs pressed closer together hoping against hope that if I pleased Jake, he'd let me taste too.

Jake's pre-cum aided him as he tilted his hips back and forth in time to the slow licks he gave to the tip of Bailey's cock. The feel of his cock gliding under my balls increased the maddening throbbing in my untouched cock.

Trapped by Jake, I was unable to look down at Bailey. "Suck my cock, Bailey, suck me now," I growled.

Wet heat surrounded my cock, and I groaned and thrust as deep as I could get. Sensations short circuited my brain and my eyelids drifted shut at the heavenly suction from Bailey's mouth.

"Sub, did I give you permission to suck Pup?" Jake demanded.

My eyes fired open, and I groaned in despair as Bailey immediately backed off. Still trapped by Jake, I couldn't see Bailey's face, but I could feel the tension rolling off him.

"No Sir...but Sam issued an order," he argued, though his voice lacked any real conviction.

"Is that so? When did Sam become the Dom in this relationship?"

A shiver raced down my body at the deep timbre of Jake's tone.

"I'm sorry, Sir." Bailey sounded utterly contrite, making me feel more than a little guilty, until I remembered how he loved Jake's punishments.

"At this rate, I'm going to need to keep a pad and pen handy to keep track of all the punishments you pair will require."

It was said so matter-of-factly, I believed every word he said, and my heart rate sped up so much I was sure Jake could feel it against his chest.

"I'll think of a suitable punishment for you both later, but right now, Bai, you can suck Sam's balls and lick my cock. Pup, I'll feed you Bailey's cock, open wide for me. But remember, you are both not to come until I say you can, understood?"

"Yes, Sir," Bailey answered, sounding very happy.

I, on the other hand, wasn't so sure about this. I was already close to the edge and unsure if sucking Bailey's cock while he sucked on my balls wouldn't have me coming in seconds. "Erm…what would happen if I shot my load before you said so?"

A wicked chuckle rumbled up Jake's chest and vibrated through me. His mouth moved to my ear and his tongue licked the rim before he whispered, "Let's hope you don't find out."

"Oh shittttt," I cried as Bailey sucked one of my balls into his hot mouth and his tongue lapped at the delicate skin. My eyes screwed shut as he released me and I panted, working on getting some semblance of control. That lasted about a second before he sucked my entire sac into his mouth, his nose nuzzling under my cock.

"Open for me, Pup," Jake growled into my ear seductively.

I struggled to lift my eyelids as my lips parted and Jake fed Bailey's cock into my mouth. The slightly bitter taste of pre-cum was followed by a richer flavour that was all Bailey. I licked the underside of his cock and the thick vein pulsed against my tongue as more bursts of pre-cum coated the inside of my mouth.

Heat and warmth surrounded me as the scent of sex filled the air. Cocooned between these two men, I lost all sense of time and place. I'd never felt so connected to one person before, never mind two. As the reality of what these two men were offering me hit fully, my body shook with overriding emotions.

Tears of joy leaked from my eyes, and then there was the feel of Jake's fingers against my lips, stopping me from choking on Bailey's cock when his hips bucked. The care Jake took to keep me safe opened my heart to the prospect that the love I held inside could grow and be shared with more than one man.

I moaned and saliva dripped from my mouth. I hollowed my cheeks to suck harder before I slid my tongue out to lick at Jake's fingers, wanting to taste him to. I wanted to have both men inside me, to be a part of me.

"Oh fuck, more...that...yeah," I muttered around Bailey's cock, not wanting to release my prize, but unable to stop myself from encouraging Bailey to continue.

Jake chuckled, then moaned deeply as my balls were released and presumably Bailey started to lick at the head of his cock.

I whimpered at the visual in my head as I licked Bailey's cock, my arse grinding back against Jake as his groin glued itself to my arse. The tug of arousal deep in my belly increased as Jake's hips rolled in a sexy move against my arse. Tiny fires spread from my balls down to my cock, and I knew it would be game over if Bailey so much as breathed on me.

As if I had transmitted that thought to Bailey, his slippery tongue ran over the base of my cock. I pulled my mouth off Bailey. "Motherfucker...shittttttttt...I'mmm sorryyyyy," I bellowed as my body bowed into Jake, my pelvis juddering as hot spurts of cum pulsed out of my cock.

In the background, I could hear Bailey ask, "Please, Sir, can I taste?" Though I didn't hear Jake's response, I soon felt Bailey swallow my cock down his throat before I'd finished coming. I panted, whined, and moaned, uncaring that I'd come without permission.

My eyelids, which must have shut, slitted open, and the second I saw Bailey's cock with a strand of pre-cum hanging from the tip, I was on him. I sucked him deep, mimicking what he did to me. As my orgasm waned, I felt Bailey stiffen, and I chuckled around his cock. Not letting up for a second, I used my tongue to lap around the mushroom head while hollowing my cheeks.

His body seemed to freeze right before he released a strangled moan, and his cock became impossibly hard. I eased back a little, wanting to taste his cum as it filled my mouth. Jake panted behind me and wet heat spread down my thigh. I groaned in delight, and as I released Bailey's cock, I twisted my head to look at Jake and slam my mouth against his, sharing my bounty.

The hand that had been feeding me Bailey's cock clasped my cheek and held me captive as Jake devoured my mouth. His tongue boldly swept over mine as he swallowed Bailey's cum. It was a hot, messy kiss, but it was fucking amazing. By the time he released me, I was grinning from ear to ear.

"I could get used to this kind of morning wake up call," I gasped, inhaling a deep breath, hoping it would get my heart rate to settle, despite Jake's dark brow arching up.

"Did I give either of you permission to cum?"

***

I shifted on my perching stool, then shifted again, trying to find a position that

116

didn't make my arse sing. The plug in my backside, that seemed to sit flush against my prostate, would have been a real pleasure to use but for one thing, I was at work!

Jake had kept to his word about punishing me for coming without permission. What I'd not expected was for him to do something that would interfere with my ability to keep a straight thought in my head at the bar. He'd been silent about what he planned to do to me, right up until I had to get ready to leave the house.

I jerked, and then groaned in distress as the plug gave my prostate a solid rub. "You okay?" Scott asked.

I shook my head, heat filling my cheeks as I eyed the busy bar and then Scott. "Jake...is an evil bastard," I ground out.

Scott's brows shot up and he glanced towards the man in question, who was stood at the far end of the bar. Jake's hand rested on Bailey's shoulder as he kneeled in a pose of submission next to him. The warmth in my face increased as my gaze was drawn to what Bailey was wearing. For his punishment, Bailey wore a collar. The lead attached to the collar was held loosely in Jake's other hand. What made me wince was the cock cage confining Bailey's dick.

I sighed, recalling how Bailey hadn't met my gaze when Jake had led him into the bar holding the lead.

Jake really knew how to deliver a punishment, that was for sure!

He'd not mentioned he'd be coming tonight, so any hope I might have had about taking out the butt plug had died the second I'd seen him. Yes, I'd wanted to take my punishment like a man, but I had my limits. The semi I'd been sporting before Jake had arrived, I could cope with, but the full-on hard-on I'd had from seeing Bailey dressed as he was...pure torment. Why had I thought being turned on was a good thing?

"There is something about him tonight that suggests he's in full Dom mode. I have to say, I've never seen him quite like this," Scott whispered before he turned his attention to the blond guy who'd sidled up to the bar. "What can I get you?"

Yeah, neither had I, and boy it was a real eye-opener. The air of confidence about him out in public was different. He fully-owned who he was and seemed proud to show off Bailey. My heart clutched. Would he be proud to show me off like that? Would I let him bring me here when I was a puppy, to show me off?

A nervous flutter started somewhere under my breastbone, so I let my gaze sweep the bar, looking for busy work. Noticing a customer holding money in their hand, I rose off the seat and took their order, happy to be distracted.

As the night wore on, I let the busy bar keep me from spending too much time dwelling on my thoughts. As the last customers left, Scott came over to me while I cleaned the bar.

"Jake is asking if I can let you go," he said, glancing back to where Jake stood.

There was no sign of Bailey, so I assumed he'd gone to get his coat to cover up.

"If you're okay with that?" Scott nodded when he glanced back at me. "Thanks, I'll owe you one."

"Cool, Luke is working late tonight and is coming to pick me up, so it's no biggie." Scott gave me a sly wink and lent into my body. "I'm sure you're about ready to beg Jake to take out whatever you've got stuck up your arse and replace it with something…else."

I blushed as Scott gave me another knowing wink and ambled off to finish emptying the tills. Had I been that obvious?

Heaving a sigh, I glanced about to make sure I'd not left anything important lying around before I walked to Jake. Every step was sheer torment as pleasure sparked inside my arse. I didn't glance down, though it was a close call as I met Jake's heavy-lidded, desire-filled gaze. A shiver ran down my spine as his eyes glinted with something dark and dangerous.

Chapter Twelve

Jake

Sam was easy to read when he came towards me. He was aroused and maybe more than a little pissed off. When he met my gaze head-on, I struggled to hide my humour. "How's my Pup doing?"

"You know damn well how I'm doing," he snarled as his chin jutted forward, his hands balled at his sides. There was a noticeable bulge in his dressy black work trousers.

"Oh, Pup, you're asking for trouble talking to me in that tone." I ran my finger down the side of his cheek. "Haven't you learnt your lesson this evening about misbehaving?" He scowled, his lips clamping together.

"Oh, it's like that is it? I think it's time to go home." His behaviour stroked at my desire. Seeing him like this, aroused with a hint of feistiness, would make it an interesting drive home.

I swallowed a chuckle, recalling how I'd left Bailey in the car. I took hold of Sam's hand. "Come on."

He came, albeit a little reluctantly, his feet dragging across the wooden floor. I kept hold of his hand until we exited the lift and stopped at the car. It was only then that he seemed to remember that Bailey had been with me. When I opened the rear door, behind the driver's side of my BMW, his mouth dropped open.

It seemed to take long seconds before he could compute what he was seeing. "Holy shit!" he squeaked. His tongue swept over his lips, his eyes becoming impossibly wide, though they never left Bailey, who was sat in the middle of the back seat of the car.

He had a black leather ball gag in his mouth and his arms had been tied behind him. His legs were splayed apart, and his ankles were attached to a spreader bar. His legs were as wide as they could stretch in the confines of the footwell. The cock cage had been removed and replaced with a cock ring, with leather straps tied around his balls after I'd stroked him to full arousal. The dark-red leather gleamed under the interior car light. His aroused cock stood proud. The tip of the clear condom I'd put on him before going to get Sam was coated with pre-cum.

I'd taken the precaution of explaining to Nathan what I was doing in case anyone was watching the security cameras. Nathan had assured me he'd man them until we left the underground car park.

Bailey had surpassed my expectations. I'd thought for sure he'd safe word when I explained what I was going to do to him in the

122

car. I'd given him a small handheld alarm to use, alerting me if he wanted to safe word. Greeted by silence in the car, I gave Bailey a warm smile. His eyes were wild and feverish, possibly from the torment of the tiny vibrating plug in his arse.

I took hold of Sam's neck in a firm grip, bringing his body flush against mine. "Look at the reward I had waiting for you. But..." I trailed off, leaving Sam to only guess as to what might happen next. I'd seen how he struggled through the evening with his desire. His needy expression had become more obvious every time he'd stared longingly at me, and Bailey's naked body.

"Oh fuck...please can't you give me a pass for once and let me have whatever you were gonna give me," he pleaded, his breathless voice barely above a whisper.

His whole body vibrated against mine and my cock throbbed. I took a few seconds to let him think I was considering his request, but I was at the end of my patience. I wanted to see him sink down on Bailey's cock, riding him while he sucked mine. After watching Sam suck Bailey's cock this morning, I'd wanted that heavenly mouth on me. With that in mind, I'd planned tonight with the same precision I used in my architecture.

Right now, though, neither man had to know how desperate I was for it to happen, after I'd spent all day visualising the three of us together in this way.

"Sam, sit on the edge of the seat next to Bailey and take off your shoes, trousers, and underwear."

His head was the only thing that moved as he looked about the garage. I could see his brow pinch. "I won't ask you again," I growled, then held my breath to see if he'd give in or safe word.

When he moved toward the car and my hand fell back to my side, I released a sharp exhale at the heat in his gaze before he sat to bend and remove his shoes. He hesitated at the sight of his prosthetic.

"Don't overthink it, Pup. I'll never put you in a position that will cause you embarrassment," I reassured him. I'd checked out the back seat, the flooring, and the space available to ensure he'd not have any difficulties with what I wanted.

"Right, like getting naked in an underground car park isn't embarrassing. You know there are security cameras. Anybody could be watching right now," he muttered, even though his hands moved to unzip his trousers. He groaned and lifted his arse to tug both the trousers and his underwear down together. His cock was dark pink and fully aroused as it jutted up from his groin, showing how much he wanted to continue.

"Yet, your cock is hard and your hands are trembling with excitement, Pup. All you need to do is safe word for this to stop."

His eyes widened, and he gave me a look that said 'don't be daft' right before he shifted on the leather seat, moaning long and loud as he did so. His cock jerked, obviously receiving a thrill of pleasure from the plug in his arse.

Realising this could be over before we started, I smacked the tip of his cock. Expecting it to dull his arousal, my eyes narrowed when his hands grappled for the base of his cock and he ringed himself. His chest heaved as sweat gathered on his top lip, his eyes screwed tightly shut.

"Fuck...that was close," he gritted out through his teeth as his eyes opened, his accusing stare meeting mine.

I tilted my head. Why had I not explored Sam's hard and soft limits? "Do you like pain, Pup?"

A deep flush spread up his neck and into his face. "I'm not sure...the throbbing in my dick after you gave it that smack...says maybe." He shrugged, and Bailey made a grunting noise, pulling my gaze from Sam to him.

His 'don't forget about me' expression was easy to read, so I gave him a devilish smirk. "Pup, let me help you straddle Bailey's lap."

Both men groaned, only Bailey shut his eyes as I chuckled. It took a little work to get Sam in between Bailey's thighs so that he could use the two headrests to hold on to. When he was situated, I asked him to lift his hips to take out the plug.

He cursed, and Bailey opened his eyes, his expression wild with need as he watched Sam's hole twitch under my touch, tantalisingly close to his face. I dropped the plug into the bag I'd brought and retrieved the lube. I slicked my fingers to a symphony of noises.

"In the name of all that is holy, hurry, hurry, hurry," Sam cried out.

Bailey grunted, mumbled around the gag, trying to move his hips closer to Sam's arse as I sank two lubed fingers in deep. I gritted my teeth as my chest billowed with the effort not to rush. By the time I'd deemed Sam ready, the air was blue with his curse words.

The second I stroked Bailey's cock with my lubed fingers, he growled at me. His forehead had deep furrows and was sheened with sweat. "Bai, you have the bell to press if this is too much." He shook his head, and I gave him a pleased smile.

"Such a good sub. Pup, sink down on my sub and ride his cock. Show him how much you want him inside you."

Bailey's eyelids drooped and his eyes filled with gratitude. Using my other hand, I stroked Bailey's cheek, feeling the warm leather of the gag against my palm. "Your submission is beautiful. You please me so much, Bai." He pushed into my hand as Sam, without any preamble, sank down on the cock I still held.

Salvia slid down Bailey's chin as he made nonsensical noises, his eyes rolling into the back of his head. Sam's arse met my hand and he groaned in delight.

"Oh fuck, feels so good inside me. I've waited forever for this. Bailey, oh Jesus, I love you," Sam cried out, his voice thick with emotions.

My heart clutched in my chest as I glanced about the garage and felt guilt twist my stomach into knots. Why didn't I plan their first time together in a more intimate setting? *Your head was too filled with giving them something unique. Yeah, that and getting to watch Bailey fuck Sam.*

Feeling the press of my zip against my cock, I pushed aside my regrets, promising myself I'd make it up to them both.

Unzipping my fly, I breathed a sigh of relief, though it only lasted a second as I watched Sam use his hold on the head rests to do as I asked, riding Bailey with a punishing rhythm. The sound of skin slapping against skin echoed off the concrete. Grunts, moans, and cries followed as I got in the car and knelt next to Bailey, cursing under my breath as I was forced to bend my head to the side to avoid hitting it on the roof. "Pup, turn your body a little towards me and lower your head. I want to feel your sweet mouth suck me."

Bailey's thigh quivered against my leather clad knees as Sam did as he was told. His lust laden expression was intoxicating as he bent sideways, still holding on with his left hand while he reached out to stroke his sweat-slicked fingers over my cock. I murmured encouragement. "Feel what belongs to you, to Bai. See how hard you both make me."

"Oh shit…if you say stuff like that, I'm gonna shoot and get into more trouble," Sam bemoaned, all the while his hungry gaze never leaving my cock.

"That's okay, Pup, this time you can come without permiss—"

"Oh, thank fuck," Sam stated before I'd finished talking. Before I could chastise him, he swallowed my cock down to the root in a move that left me reeling. Didn't he have a gag reflex?

The question flew right out of my head as he tongued my cock and hollowed his cheeks. My toes curled in my boots, the powerful suction leaving none of my body untouched. Tiny fires of arousal pulsed through my body. The hairs on my skin stood up and I moaned at the sheer pleasure taking me on a trip straight to heaven. His mouth was wicked and destroyed my control.

My hips bucked and my balls tingled as I strained to keep control, wanting this to last more than a minute. The cacophony of sounds, and the scent of musky bodies and leather worked to shred my sanity. Then I looked at Bailey and it was over, all bar the shouting. His face was lax and there was heavy-lidded desire stamped into his features. His naked chest was slick with sweat as he met each of Sam's jerky movements. I lifted my hands, needing to connect the three of us. I placed my hand on Bailey's chest, over his heart, and cupped Sam's cheek. "You're so perfect together."

Sam met my gaze as he cried out. The vibration spread up my cock and shocked my balls into releasing their bounty into his willing mouth. As I shuddered and gasped, Bailey groaned around the gag long and loud as Sam slammed himself down and started to tremble. We seemed to be suspended for seconds as we all found our pleasure together.

My heart soared with joy, and I struggled to keep control of the emotions raging through me, desperate to declare aloud that these men were mine. To demand they…love me too. A shudder wracked my body as I sucked in some much-needed air.

When Sam released my cock, he looked down at his lap and then back at Bailey. "Well, that's another fine mess you got me into Bailey."

Laughter filled the car as Bailey sagged against the leather and struggled to grin around the gag. *God these men were priceless.*

Chapter Thirteen

*B*ailey

Watching the sky brighten through the blinds, I sighed quietly, knowing it was pointless to stay in bed when I couldn't shut my head off. Untangling myself from Sam's sleeping form, I slipped out of the warm bed, holding my breath.

A glance at Jake confirmed that he was still sound asleep, so I crept out of the bedroom and headed to my old room. Only once the door was shut behind me did I release the air trapped in my chest. I stood and stared unseeingly at the room that had been mine for the past few months.

So much had changed over the last few days that I just needed a moment to process on my own. Last night had been on replay through my head and had kept me awake all night. Whatever my expectations had been about being in a threesome that allowed me to submit twenty-four-seven, it hadn't been this. I'd never felt so far out of my element, yet it was as if a vital part of me, that I'd not known was missing, had been returned.

When Jake had asked me to accompany him to Flamingo Bar yesterday, it had been with trepidation that I'd accepted. I'd known he planned to punish both me and Sam for coming without permission. What I'd not considered was how clever Jake was in devising his punishments.

First there was the cock cage he'd put on me before he'd had Sam bend in front of me to put a plug into his arse before he went to work. Sam's smug look had died when he'd stood and the thing had shifted in his arse. His semi-hard cock was obvious when he dressed in his work trousers. He'd left looking miserable, while Jake had been grinning from ear to ear.

Then Jake had requested I wear a collar and leash for the evening when we went to the bar. I'd known I could safe word, but with the look of expectation on his face, that had quickly been followed by approval when I'd agreed, albeit reluctantly, was hard to resist.

All the years of being a sub hadn't quite prepared me for how these two men could twist me into the knots. I'd understood that Jake was testing me, and that the evening had been all about me showing Jake that I was his and Sam's.

What with Sam's hungry eyes following my every move, it had been a sensual experience that made me glad of the cock cage. Otherwise, I'd been certain I'd have come again without permission. Why was it so hard to keep control around these two men?

They're yours, stop questioning everything.

My jaw ached as my teeth clenched together at my body's response to how Jake had proved just that in the underground car park. A fluttering started under my breastbone at how Jake had apologised for what he felt he'd deprived me and Sam of—a bed for our first time together.

I chuckled. A bed was the last thing I'd wanted after Jake had explained to me in great detail what was going to happen after he brought Sam to the car. At that point, he could have laid me on the garage floor and demanded that I let people watch as Sam sank down on my cock. I wouldn't have cared in the slightest. Sam had claimed me in front of Jake, displaying his own vulnerabilities to do it, and if I weren't already so deeply in love with him, I'd have fallen right then.

And wasn't that why I'd not slept? This need to please these two men, to give them all of me, even if it left me vulnerable, was huge. It was bigger than the need I'd felt for years to please my father. With him dead, I had no way of proving that I'd have stood up to him for my men, but I knew deep inside I'd do absolutely anything for these men, regardless of the cost to me. Jake had given me courage to accept me, to accept my feelings for Sam.

The feelings I had for Sam had developed over time, they'd kind of crept up on me. They were more mellow and hummed through me like a blow heater on constant. Jake was a whole different ball game, and I was starting to understand that they were as vital as my feelings for Sam, even if they were different. They were intense and scary as fuck, given how fast he'd slipped into my head and my heart.

The very same heart skipped a beat as I swung around, doing my best to conceal my thoughts as the handle of the door rattled before it swung open. Jake stood in the doorway, naked and very distracting. His honey smooth skin tempted me to lick as my gaze moved up his body, resting finally on his face. There was something so alluring about him. He was attractive, there was no doubting that, but there was an inner quality that called to me.

His eyes crinkled at the edges, concern in their depths. "Was yesterday too much?"

The straightforwardness was something I appreciated, even when it was difficult to answer. "I...yes and no...I was thinking about my...feelings." At the latter, I dipped my gaze anxiously, fear gripping me by the throat.

His bare feet appeared in front of me and his hand came into view before it gently encouraged me to look at him. I might have been taller and broader than him, but his dominance always made me feel he was the bigger man. A shiver of desire ran through me.

His eyes were warm and compassionate. "I should have been more considerate about the choice of venue, I'm sorry. The scene was intense, and it's bound to leave you feeling a little out of sorts after all those years of wanting Sam."

A band constricted my chest as he brushed my cheek with his fingertips in a gentle gesture that opened my heart a little more to him. His demand for honesty rang through me as I kept hold of his gaze. "The place was irrelevant. And it's not just being with Sam, it's you too."

His head tilted to the side as he looked up at me with a now unreadable expression. "Is that good or...bad?" His hesitation, and the slight tremor in his voice, were the only indication he was worried.

"Good...well, it's good if you like me." Fiery heat filled my neck and face as I cringed inwardly at how dorky I sounded. It was almost as if I'd reverted to being the fourteen-year-old boy who asks his first crush if they like him.

His pupils seemed to take up the whole of his irises as he stepped into my body, the heat from him making me feel instantly warm. His breath touched my lips as his palm slid over my ear and around the back of my head in a possessive move. "I more than like you, Bai. The same goes for the sleeping man in the next room. You both are precious to me."

His lips gently pressed against mine in a fleeting kiss. "Let's go wake up Pup, have a shower, and I'll treat you both to breakfast and we can talk about last night."

I nodded eagerly. Naked shower time with my two men? I could get behind that. Talking...that could wait.

***

The following week, I'd found that Jake loved to talk, *a lot*. He felt the need to make us talk about everything we did together. It was a little weird as I'd never had a Dom do that before, but I got his reasoning behind it. He wanted open honesty to prevent any misconceptions or anyone feeling left out, especially when we went into his playroom. That, unfortunately, hadn't been as often as I'd like. As we'd settled into a loose kind of routine, Jake's organisational skills had come to the fore. With Sam's schedule at the bar and Jake's job, it made it difficult to find time for all three of us to be together. So Jake had bought a calendar for everyone to put their plans for the week on, so we could identify time we could all be together more easily.

It turned out, I was the only one with no plans, not that I minded after years of having all my time dictated for me. Only, that left me on my own a lot, with too much time on my hands to think.

"You're brooding, Sarge, what's up?" Nathan asked bluntly as I blinked him back into focus.

How long had I been sitting staring into space?

I eyed Nathan. "I've been considering looking for a job. With Jake and Sam working full-time, it leaves me at a loose end." I shrugged when Nathan's gaze turned thoughtful.

"What have you been doing this last week?"

I hesitated and thought about the shopping I'd bought to make meals for my guys when they got home, tired and hungry. Then there was the washing and ironing, and some general household cleaning just to keep on top of things. Three people in a house could create quite a bit of mess when one of them was Sam. The guy was untidy, and often forgot where he'd put stuff because he left it lying around everywhere. As Jake liked the place tidy, I played peacekeeper and tidied up. Am I a house husband?

Nathan laughed. "You've just figured out you have a full-time job already keeping your men happy. I'm right, aren't I?" He pointed at me as I went to deny it and the heat in my face gave me away.

"Yes, you are. So what?" I asked huffily.

The leather of Nathan's office chair creaked as he sat forward, his face showing nothing but happiness. "So nothing. You have exactly what you've always craved. Someone, or now, two someones that allow you to just be yourself. You were always the sergeant people went to for advice, for support, because you like to take care of people. That was regardless of the fact you could be a hard-nosed bastard when it was called for. People were drawn to your gentle nature. I got it, the guys, possibly not so much because you used the dominant act as a shield. Being a Dom, I saw beneath it. I think you should stop questioning what you've been lucky to find and just run with it and see where it leads."

His words rang through my head. I walked into Jake's home office two hours later. "Do you have a few minutes?" I asked from the doorway. When Jake worked from home, I tried to not interrupt him.

He laid down his pen and gave me his full attention. Something else I was coming to...*love*. My innards turned to jelly as I lowered my gaze.

"What's up, Bai?"

"Do you think I should get a job?" Not quite the question I wanted to ask, but with my nerves trying to kick my backside, it was what came out.

"Look at me, Bai." His deep, husky demand caused a shiver of desire to run through me as I did as he bid without hesitation. "You do a lot in our home, is that not enough to satisfy you?"

"I love what I do for you and Sam."

"Then what is the issue?"

This time I shuddered at the dominance he was displaying. "I didn't want to assume the role of house...sub...when maybe you wanted me to do something more productive," I stuttered and stumbled, while embarrassment jogged at my heels. Where had the confident sergeant gone? I nearly rolled my eyes at my own ridiculousness.

Jake pushed back his seat, his stare the only indication of what he wanted. Wordlessly, I walked to the side of his chair and knelt in a pose of submission. Once I'd settled, he shifted, his hand stroking over my head causing me to whimper. Pushing into the soft touch, a pleasurable sigh followed. His hand moved to my shoulders. His fingers dug into the tight muscles as he massaged me.

I groaned and relaxed.

"I want whatever makes you happy. That is the only important thing. Think about it—"

"I don't need to, Sir. I want to look after you and Sam full-time."

He tutted at my interruption but didn't call me out. "Then you have your answer."

The warmth that came from his easy acceptance left me a little breathless, but also filled me with a contentedness that I was coming to understand was a frequent feeling in this new life.

Chapter Fourteen

Sam

Glasses clinked as one of the circulating waiters took the full tray of drinks to the booth right next to the stage. A stage I'd avoided looking at because tonight was solely aimed at those who liked being a puppy. There must have been two dozen men wearing puppy gear. The scent of arousal was heady tonight with so much naked flesh on show as men displayed their puppies for others to admire.

As far as my men were concerned, tonight was just like any other at the bar because I'd not mentioned what was happening to either of them. Jake had had to go away this morning and wouldn't be returning until tomorrow night. I'd tried to fool myself into believing that was why I'd not mentioned what was happening tonight to him. His trip away was a last-minute thing, so the only person I was kidding was myself.

"Sam, I need six of this week's craft beer for table seven," Theo said, his voice raised to be heard over the chatter and music.

I glanced at Theo's grinning face and nodded. He'd been pulled in tonight because one of the regular waiters had called in sick half-an-hour before the event was due to start. As tonight was a ticketed event, we'd known we'd never cope with one man down. Scott had made a quick call to Theo, knowing it was his day off from La Trattoria Di Amore. After bribing him with double the hourly rate, he'd happily agreed to dig us out of a sticky situation.

"On it." I spun around, forgetting myself for a second, and staggered into Scott. "Shit, sorry." I blushed as Scott helped me regain my footing.

"No problem. I'm a clumsy fool, ask anyone," Scott said, giving me a wink.

"Ain't that the truth. Remember when you poured that drink all over Luke?" Theo said through his laughter.

Scott shrugged, his cheeks blooming with colour. "That may or may not have been an accident." He glanced at me. "We weren't together then, and Luke often liked to make me cry."

My eyes widened. "Seriously?"

"Oh hell yeah, they had a real love/hate thing going on for about two years till Scott ended up on a blind date with Luke after using The App," Theo explained, while Scott scowled at him.

Forgetting about what I was doing, I leaned against the bar. "How come you guys never mentioned this before? You met

142

through The App, that's how I met Jake," I offered up, hoping to ease some of Scott's embarrassment.

"You've got like an app club going on here. I feel totally left out right now," Theo sighed dramatically, a smile on his lips. Yet there was something flickering in his eyes that said he was telling the truth, that he did indeed feel left out.

"Download it. You got nothing to lose, have you?" I shrugged and stood tall when another waiter came to the bar with a drinks order. "Time to get back to work, these customers won't serve themselves...unfortunately."

I filled Theo's order and the next four, using it as a diversion when I found my gaze moving against my will back to the stage again and again. The guy currently on display had similar leather gear to mine.

Squinting to see if his was handcrafted like mine, I gave a little snort. The mask fit well but it wasn't moulded to his upper face like mine. His collar was beautiful though. It had little stones decorating it and they glittered under the spotlights that shone down on him. The guy's tail was plaited in several braids and he swished it a few times when his master tugged on his lead. His aroused cock hung between his legs and a strand of pre-cum hung suspended on its tip.

143

I shifted my gaze away as a flood of regret that I'd never get to be displayed in this way hit me. My lungs seemed to seize and keep hold of the air I'd inhaled. I walked to the back of the bar and started to tidy up some of the bottles, to work on getting my breath back. It hurt to look at what I'd once wanted with a master.

A hand touched my shoulder, and I glanced back at Scott. "You okay?" His brow was furrowed, and his black eyebrows disappeared under his floppy fringe.

"No, not really," I blurted out, then sighed when Scott looked down at my leg and back at my face. Scott was aware that my kink was puppy play, and his face was full of sympathy.

"We can't talk now, but what about tomorrow? We could go for a drink before we start work. I'm a good listener and I promise I can keep a secret if there's a need."

"I'd like that," I answered without hesitation.

***

The next morning, as I sat opposite Scott in Freshly Squeezed, I didn't feel as confident about talking about my worries.

"Drink up. You're gonna love the supersonic smoothie," Scott enthused before he took a large gulp of his own drink.

144

He'd talked me into getting an ice cream based smoothie with Nutella, apple, banana, pineapple, blueberries, and honey. I eyed the brownish liquid with trepidation as I lifted the heavy glass that looked like an old mason jar, but with a handle. I sniffed, finding the smell inoffensive, before I took a tiny sip. The creamy chocolate flavour burst over my tongue as the fruitiness followed. I groaned and took a larger mouthful. "This is bloody yummy."

Scott grinned. "I told you it was good. Gareth sure knows how to make a great smoothie." Scott gave the guy behind the counter a happy grin before he focused back on me. "Now you know you like the smoothie; you can stop avoiding telling me what's on your mind." Scott's voice became serious.

"You know that me, Bailey, and Jake are together?" Scott nodded. "Jake has his own playroom and over the last couple of weeks, we've played together a few times." A blush rode up my cheeks as Scott shifted closer to the table. "Since the very first time we were together, Jake hasn't asked me to be a puppy again."

"He's excluding you. That's so not cool, man." Scott's indignation was loud enough for several heads to turn in our direction.

"Keep it down," I hissed, and he hunched. "He's not excluding me. Jake isn't like that. I'm very much a part of what happens between him and Bailey. It's his rule there is no play without all of us being present. And it's working. It's just that since Bailey found us in the playroom before things were resolved between us—"

"Hang on, you've lost me, go back. What do you mean before things were resolved between you?"

Scott frowned, and I rolled my eyes, recalling he wasn't fully aware of my past with Bailey. So I quickly ran through how I knew Bailey and my feelings for him.

"Holy fuck, man, that's a tough ride you had there. I thought my rocky start with Luke was bad. That pales in comparison to you and Bailey. That must have sucked when he didn't acknowledge his real feelings. It must have been hard to forgive him and move on. You're a good man, Sam." His voice was full of sympathy.

I nodded, unable to speak with a ball clogging my throat.

He reached out and touched my hand, the chill from his icy fingers reminding me that I was still clutching my smoothie in my other hand. I took a drink and swallowed deep, hoping it would ease the tightness in my throat.

"So what do you think is stopping Jake from asking you to be a puppy?"

"I'm not sure. At first, I thought it was because he was looking to make Bailey feel more comfortable submitting. He struggled in the beginning, to let go fully. Thing is, over this last week, something has changed, and Bailey is acting submissive all the time. So now I think it's something else."

I sucked in a shaky breath before asking, "What if now Jake has Bailey, he doesn't need me being a puppy for him?" The pain that accompanied the voicing of my fears sliced deep, and I fought to keep inside the sob that rose up my throat. I'd avoided acknowledging how much that would hurt. I just hadn't expected it to cause so much pain.

The pressure on my hand increased and I realised I'd shifted my gaze to the table. I looked up at Scott through blurry eyes, meeting his compassionate gaze. "You need to talk to Jake. If you say he's all about openness and honesty, then he'll want to know his actions are hurting you. The three of you have a deep connection. Any fool can see that. Don't let that go because of a misunderstanding."

Scott's eyes clouded for a second before a smile formed on his lips. "Maybe talking is overrated. Maybe you'd be better showing them both what they're missing. I bet you look hot as a puppy."

Scott's confidence boost buoyed me through the day, so much so that when I got home that night, I immediately checked out the calendar. I fist-pumped the air, seeing we were all home the following evening and Jake had written 'date night'.

A smile formed on my face. *Perfect.*

Chapter Fifteen

$\mathcal{J}$ake

Hearing footsteps approach my office, I looked up from the drawing in front of me.

"Jake, how's the new design coming along for Richardson's new home?" my father asked as he stepped through my open office door. His presence dominated the room as he walked to the brown leather seat opposite my desk.

The grey Hugo Boss suit fitted his lean frame and matched the tie he wore with a white shirt that I was sure would be Hugo Boss too. My father was nothing if not predictable. He'd been a fan of the designer for years, and I wasn't sure he'd worn any other designer's clothes since he'd discovered their label.

I inhaled his expensive aftershave as he relaxed back in the chair and I met his questioning gaze. "It's coming. At this point, the man has changed his mind no less than four times. I'm still not sure he knows exactly what he wants."

"He's paying for the privilege, so who are we to complain."

I arched my brow. "That might be the case, but if he's changing his mind that often,

I have to delay other projects to go back down to Wales and fix the designs because he's no good at explaining what he wants." There was no heat in my response, only frustration as I sat forward and dropped my pen, running my hands through my hair.

Mr. Richardson lived in a remote part of Wales, which meant I'd had to stay overnight. Sam had got upset the second time I'd had to go, claiming he couldn't sleep without me being in the bed. It warmed my heart but left me feeling edgy at not being able to give him what he wanted all the time.

Was that why he hadn't slept last night? Was he worried I'd need to go away again?

Sam's place in the bed was between me and Bailey. He liked to lay half on Bailey with me spooning his back. The three of us seemed to have adapted to the sleeping arrangements much easier than I'd anticipated, so I was all the more aware that something was bothering him last night when he'd fidgeted for most of it. He usually snuggled in, found his spot, and instantly fell asleep after coming in late from work.

Last night, he'd not done that, and then this morning he'd been silent. It wasn't like him, and when he'd left for work, the kiss he'd given me felt like he was distracted.

"—those benefit the company, Jake, and they never bothered you before, so what's changed?"

My father's pencil-thin brows rose, and I struggled to recall what we'd been talking about...Richardson. "I know that it benefits the company." When my Father nodded, I breathed a little easier. "It's just that..." I trailed off, trying to figure out how to bring up my personal situation.

My parents were aware I was gay. I'd come out when I was seventeen, and since then, they'd never spoken about it. It wasn't that they displayed any unhappiness about it, they just didn't discuss personal stuff. It was just their way. They were old-fashioned and never pried into my personal life and I'd accepted it. I also felt partly to blame as I'd chosen not to take any of my previous boyfriends to meet them.

"It's just what?" my Father prompted, his forehead developing deep furrows.

"I've *boyfriends* that don't like me leaving them," I muttered truthfully, stressing the plural in boyfriends.

The furrows deepened and his brows met as he gave me a look I couldn't read. "As in two? Isn't that a little distasteful? I never considered you would feel it was acceptable to cheat on a partner." His voice was full of condemnation.

"Dad, I'm not cheating on either man. They both live with me and share my bed," I said rather bluntly, and then regretted it as he visibly blanched.

"You've two partners…isn't that…" he trailed off as he coughed.

"Complicated?" He nodded, his face draining of colour. "Yes, but you've taught me that communication and honesty are key things in any relationship. I've applied those principles to all my relationships, this is no different. Bailey and Sam…they are special men and I have feelings for both of them."

An uncomfortable look crossed his face before he released what sounded like a resigned sigh. "As long as you're happy, that was all your mother and I have ever wanted for you."

The truth was there on his concerned face, and I had to blink back the sudden rush of tears that filled my eyes. "I know, Dad. They make me very happy." I sucked in a fortifying breath before asking, "Would you like to meet them?"

His nod was immediate. "Of course, but let me warn your mother first."

"Yeah, that might be a good idea," I chuckled. My mother was prone to theatrics when faced with too much change at once, which was part of the reason they had no idea I was a Dom. I swallowed the next chuckle as my father went back to discussing Richardson and my other projects, dropping the subject.

When I left the office later that afternoon, I felt lighter and wondered how to approach my guys about going to my parents' house for dinner. Would Sam's past experience, or lack of parents, make him think twice about saying yes to dinner with mine?

I frowned as I got in my car, parked in the underground car park that was situated under the building. I plonked my briefcase down on the seat next to me and rested my head on the steering wheel, overwhelmed by my feelings at the lack of love Sam had suffered as a child.

Although he'd glossed over his time in foster care that first week we'd spent getting to know each other, he'd struggled to keep his emotions in check, showing he was not as unaffected as he'd stated. My heart had bled for him as he'd tried to brush it off like it didn't matter. The only real connection he'd mentioned was with one of his foster carer's dogs, Quinn. There was love and affection as he spoke about the German Pointer. This insight into his past had given me a better understanding as to why he possibly liked to be a puppy.

He'd never been given the same love and affection I'd had from humans; he'd only got that from a dog. Fuck, even Bailey's father, who'd been a pushy sod, had not been afraid to show his love for Bailey. It had left me trying to figure out how to give Sam what he needed without him being a puppy.

Had Sam noticed I'd not asked him to be a puppy? He'd not mentioned it. Was that a good thing? Nerves fluttered in my belly. Did he understand I wanted him whether he was being a puppy for me or not?

Questions circulated around my head as I headed home and the busy traffic kept me occupied, making me later than I'd planned to be. I sent up a prayer that I hadn't ruined dinner. Bailey's habit of having a meal ready for when I'd got home was something I truly appreciated after a long day in the office.

There had been a positive switch in Bailey's behaviour as he accepted what he'd hidden from for so long, being a full-time submissive. Since our conversation the week before, he'd all but glowed with happiness as he took care of me and Sam. Every day my feelings deepened for him while I watched him embrace who he was.

Sam had a few raised eyebrow moments when Bailey decided to kneel on the floor next to me on the rare evenings we'd all sit to watch TV, though had said nothing about it. Instead, he'd shown his support by scooting closer to me on the sofa so he could reach across my lap to stroke Bailey's hair, which he'd started to let grow. It was at the standing up phase and was silky soft to the touch, and the sexy-as-fuck silver streaks were becoming more obvious. He truly was a silver-haired fox.

My cock plumped at the memory of holding those silky strands this morning while Bailey had sucked my cock and Sam had sucked Bailey's. "Driving and sexy thoughts don't mix," I muttered, cursing as I clenched my thighs together, willing the image out of my head as I took the last turning that led me to my home.

I gave a grateful sigh as I pulled into my parking space without incident. It was getting harder and harder not to think about my men and what came next. Besides the night in the garage where Sam had fucked Bailey, I'd restrained myself from what I wanted, needing them both to be comfortable with what was happening between us. They were being led by me, and after the hurt Bailey had unwittingly inflicted on Sam in the past, I wanted them to find their way through those hurts before I did more with them in the bedroom.

I heaved a sigh at how much the waiting was killing me and collected my briefcase. I exited the car, locked it, and headed up the path to the house. Glancing up at my home, I faltered at the flood of happiness that came with the knowledge of what waited for me beyond the front door.

I sucked in a shaky breath at the rush of giddy excitement that was accompanied by constant butterflies that told me how deep I was falling for both men. I'd wake daily, feeling like I could take on the world. I might not have put a name to my feelings, *yet,* but I knew what I felt for these men deep inside my heart. It was life-changing and I wanted it more than I'd wanted anything I'd ever worked towards in my life. It was scary that my happiness was connected to not one, but two men.

Can a person have it all?

My hands shook when the notion ran on repeat as I opened my front door. I stepped in, shut the door, and placed my briefcase down before removing my shoes. I tilted my head to the side and listened harder. Was there someone in the playroom?

Would Bailey and Sam defy my rule about us all being present to play together?

My heart slammed against my ribs as I stood tall, the giddy feeling I had outside replaced with a sense of dread. As I walked to the partially open door and pushed it, my dream seemed to slip out of my grasp.

Chapter Sixteen

*B*ailey

"I'm tellin' you, this is not a good idea," I grumbled, even as I knelt in front of Sam after he'd sat in the armchair in the playroom, naked as a jaybird. He'd showered and the scent of pomegranate wafted from his bare skin. His tanned body was smooth, and his muscles rippled, tantalising me to do more than remove his prosthetic limb.

With trembling fingers, I carefully followed the instructions Sam had previously given me on how to safely take off his titanium leg. The times he allowed me to care for him in this way were precious and filled my heart to capacity with love for him. The occasions when he'd refuse for me to touch it, especially when it was giving him pain, had hurt. Then I'd thought about how I'd feel and gone off to do a little research about amputees and what it was like for them. There was a lot of information about how it weirded some people out when someone touched their stump, or even the space where the limb had once been. Sam wasn't so much bothered about that, not when he spent so much time pressed up against me when he slept.

"Yes, I know. I heard you the first fifty times you said it since I suggested it. But I need to know that he accepts me too."

The deflated way he spoke and looked as he eyed me, left me with no option but to help him. My heart wouldn't allow me to do anything else, regardless of the punishment Jake was sure to dish out when he found us in here without him.

When Sam had come home an hour ago and talked about how upset he was, I'd wanted to fix it. Although I'd tried to convince him to wait for Jake to come home, he wouldn't listen. He'd somehow got it into his head that Jake didn't need or want him because he had me. Was I to blame for Sam feeling like this, by submitting to Jake fully?

A band of uncertainty cinched around my chest, restricting my air flow. "I'm sorry. I've caused this, haven't I?" My fingers lay against the metal as I glanced up under my eyelashes, frightened at what he might say.

He sat forward and his hands cupped my cheeks, bringing my gaze to his. "No, you haven't. Jake has—"

"Jake has what?" came the steely demand from the doorway.

A wild buzzing started in my ears as Sam's hands fell to his lap when he glanced towards the door. I sucked in a fortifying breath before I looked at Jake. None of us spoke. For a moment, the waves of dominance that came off Jake made it difficult for me to form a sentence.

Sam pulled himself together way quicker than me. "Why haven't you asked me to be a puppy?"

I could feel the heat drain from my face at the anger in Sam's accusation and watched Jake flinch, and then indicate with his finger between me and Sam.

"Is that what this is all about? Were you going to be a puppy for Bailey without me?" His voice was tight and controlled, much like his expression, and my heart sank at how my worries we'd fuck up became a reality.

Crap, I should have got Sam to listen to reason. Would he have listened to you? I mean, come on, how many times did you tell him this was a bad idea?

Nerves danced over my skin, giving me the urge to scratch at myself as Jake stood stock still, waiting for Sam to answer. I braced when Sam started to visibly shake in front of me.

"What! Are you for fucking real right now? We all made a pact not to play in this room without everyone being present." His arm came up and nearly slapped me in the face, but thankfully I was quick enough to dodge it as his hand swept the room. "Do we look like we're playing without you? Were you not the one who wrote *'date night'* on the calendar?"

His eyes snapped with temper as he shifted his gaze from Jake to me. "Could he be any more dense?"

There was a shocked, angry hiss, and I shook my head at Sam, thinking he might have just overstepped the mark by a bloody mile with that parting shot. A part of me wanted to say something, but I sucked my lip in between my teeth and bit it to keep quiet. Jake and Sam needed to have this conversation to clear up whatever confusion lay between them.

"It would appear I am, so you'll have to spell it out for me," Jake answered, his voice lacking all emotion.

Sam's chest heaved, but he didn't back down. "I'm not a cheater. I'm a man of my word and it hurts that you think differently." He licked at his lips, his shoulders stiffening. "That's the first thing. The second thing is, since the very first time I dressed as a puppy, you've not once asked me to play. Yes, you've included me, and I've played with you and Bailey, but it's like you've been giving Bailey everything he needs and forgot about...me." As he finished speaking, his voice dropped to a mere whisper, but the hurt I could hear was all but suffocating.

I was fast, but Jake was faster as we both reached for Sam at the same time. He didn't push me away, instead he wrapped his arms around the pair of us, sandwiching Sam between us. Sam buried his head in Jake's chest while his hand clutched at my T-shirt. "I'm sorry I'm not enough for you both," he sobbed inconsolably.

"Oh fuck," Jake ground out, sounding devastated by Sam's confession. His chest expanded and deflated twice before he released us and got down on the floor next to me. He glanced between us both and gave a defeated sigh.

"Let's clear a few things up. I…think…no, that's wrong. I *know* I love you both. I also know it's possibly too soon to declare those feelings when it's not been more than a month since we started this relationship. But my feelings are strong, *for both of you.* Let's make that very clear.*"

He loves us! Holy mother of God!

When Sam glanced from Jake to me and back, the hand holding my T-shirt turned white-knuckled. Jake put a finger against Sam's lips as they parted. "No, I'm not finished. I want you to listen and hear what I say. I'm a fool. When you talked about your past and Quinn the dog, I thought that by not asking you to be a puppy, you'd see what I felt for you was real."

My lips quivered as Sam's eyes flooded with fresh tears. They silently rolled down his cheeks and dripped off his quivering chin as Jake continued. "Now I can see that was a mistake. I've made you think I wasn't interested, but that couldn't be further from the truth. I fucked up. There was me asking you both for honesty and I wasn't giving you the same courtesy. I won't make the same mistake again," he finished, giving a resigned sigh.

"I'm sorry for speaking out of turn," Sam said sheepishly, his cheeks getting a rosy glow to them as he looked at me with red-rimmed eyes. "I should have listened to you."

Jake's face formed into a smile for the first time since he'd stepped into the room. He wiped the tears tracking down Sam's face. "So Bailey tried to reason with you, did he, Pup?"

Sam nodded, his breathing increasing.

Jake, after he'd finished wiping Sam's face, moved one hand to the back of Sam's neck, holding him still before looking directly at me. "What say we let Pup have a play before we eat?"

I was about to answer when Jake's eyes fired with a wickedness I'd come to recognise when he embraced his Dom fully, and the words died on my lips. Sam vibrated with happiness, but I braced for what was coming.

"In fact, let's take Sam's puppy gear upstairs and, Bai, you can help dress Pup before you plate-up dinner. I'll just need to grab a few things from my cabinet, so Pup here isn't able to come...before we've had a chance *to play with him.*"

I squirmed at the images filling my head. The way Sam grinned, I got the impression he'd not heard the veiled threat Jake had just issued. *Oh, this will be interesting!*

Chapter Seventeen

Sam

I was still reeling from Jake's confession, so I didn't fully comprehend the meaning behind what he'd just said. A feeling I might have missed something grew when Bailey looked at me with sympathy and what looked a bit like envy. What had I missed?

Jake didn't give me a chance to ask, immediately getting up and going to the cabinets housing all his things. My brow arched at Bailey, but he just shook his head while his lips twitched.

"Take Sam upstairs, Bai, and help him get dressed while I have a quick shower."

There was no room for argument against the dominance in his voice. As it was, Bailey was already obeying Jake and was checking my prosthetic was secure before standing to help me up. He then grabbed my bag containing my puppy gear once I was steady on my feet.

His gaze dropped to my arousal and his nostrils flared as deep colour spread over his cheekbones. The warmth in the room increased with the sexual tension escalating between us. It made me feel a little light-headed, so I was glad Bailey took hold of my arm and guided me out of the room and up the stairs to the third floor. There was a rich scent of meat cooking as we crested the top of the stairs, but I was too excited to think about eating right then.

It all felt a little like a dream, only my aching eyes reminded me it wasn't. A wave of embarrassment heated my cheeks at the meltdown and accusations I'd thrown at Jake, of things I'd been guilty of myself. I'd not spoken honestly about how I was feeling, when all he'd been trying to do was prove he cared about me.

"Don't over think it. You've talked about it now. It's all out in the open, he's apologised."

"Yeah, but I still feel shitty for not asking him outright what the issue was. Then I called him dense," I complained mournfully as I looked up at Bailey.

"Oh, I don't think you'll need to worry about that. I'm quite sure Jake will have a plan to make you pay for that little misdemeanour."

My heart took flight at the devilish twinkle in Bailey's eyes. "Oh shit! What do you think he's gonna do to me?"

Bailey's rich laughter filled the room. "What we're going to do to you, Pup."

He tugged me carefully over to the sofa and his gaze dipped again to the glistening head of my cock protruding between my thighs as I sat down. The temptation to stroke myself caused me to grip the cushions on either side of me. "You want to taste me, Bai?"

He shuddered and his bulge, that was now eye level in front of me in his low hanging sweatpants, increased. "I do, but only if Jake lets me."

There was resignation in his voice, that didn't hurt my ego in the slightest, as he said nothing more and got back on his knees to finish what he'd started in the playroom before Jake had arrived home.

I sat trembling as he removed my prosthetic with sure hands. The care he took to make sure he did as I'd previously instructed when he'd asked how he could help me, was breath-taking. My arousal increased with each gentle touch as he slipped on first my mask, then my knee pads and gloves.

When he went back into the bag, he paused and glanced back at me. "You've a collar in here, and a lead. The first time you were with Jake, I don't remember you wearing them." His brows rose as if he were searching his memory.

"No, I wasn't. They show a sign of possession when you give them to your master. I wasn't sure, at the time, I wanted Jake to be my master...or anyone else, other than you," I confessed truthfully.

"What about now?" Bailey lifted the collar and lead up and held them out to me.

His gaze was steady on mine. There was a world of want in his eyes. "Why don't you put them on me, Bai."

A huge grin spread over his face as he shifted a little closer and I lowered my head for ease. The feel of the cool leather touching my neck left me feeling oddly at peace. He fastened the buckles at the front of my neck before he attached the lead. He tugged a little and I yipped for him before he dropped the leather leash.

Bailey's controlled desire was intoxicating as he slipped on my mask. Hot breaths touched my naked skin as he checked everything was in place. Lastly, he lifted the tail I'd chosen for today. It had a good-sized plug that had several bumps on it that would give me a great internal massage when I moved over the floor.

It was my favourite...*oh shit!* Jake's words came back to me. *I'll just need to grab a few things from my cabinet, so Pup here isn't able to come...before we've had a chance to play with him.*

What did he mean by that?

I glanced worriedly at Bailey who was busy lubing the plug. "I don't think I need the tail," I squeaked in alarm.

"Don't be silly. Of course, you need your tail, Pup," came Jake's deep, husky voice, that sounded as if he'd drunk a bucket load of honey, from the other side of the room.

As I swung my head around to face him, the air left my lungs in a whoosh. He was naked and fully aroused. His cock curved up towards his abdomen from the dark trimmed hair at the base. His hair was still damp from the shower and brushed back off his forehead. His eyes were feverish as they swept over me. Dark-red patches of colour filled his cheeks. The tension in his body was visible in the slight trembling of his lean muscles.

He was stunningly masculine, and the air of dominance only added to the churning need growing inside me to get down on the floor and beg him to fuck me. Bailey made a whimpering sound in the back of his throat and I glanced at him. He looked in no better condition to me as he clutched the plug in his hand as if he'd lost the ability to move.

"Come to me, Pup."

I didn't need to be asked twice, I got down onto my knees and crawled to him, moving my hips enticingly, giving both men a show.

"Sub, give me the tail and then strip."

I swallowed hard as Bailey walked around me and handed the tail over to Jake, not moving away and remaining where he was to strip right next to me. It left me just below the eyeline of his cock. His bare balls hung heavy and I licked my lips, imagining the weight of them in my mouth.

"You want to nibble on our sub's balls, Pup?"

I yapped and nuzzled at Jake's bare thigh, putting his cock temptingly close to my nose. The scent of his freshly washed skin was all I could smell. His hand stroked down my spine and landed on my tailbone. He rubbed gentle circles over my arse cheeks before his warm finger slipped between my arse cheeks, teasing my rim. I lapped at his fresh-scented leg as he teased and played with me.

The pressure against my hole increased before he pressed the dry tip of his finger inside. The burn was immediate but with it came a surge of pleasure. He didn't push any deeper, just let me get used to the feeling. I groaned in disappointment a few seconds later when he slipped back out, only to exhale loudly when he returned, replacing his finger with the lubed tip of the plug.

Ohhhhhhh!

He spread the lube over my sensitive skin, using the plug to rub it into my arse. "Bear down, Pup."

I did as he requested, my pulse skipping madly. I started to pant as he sank the plug in without hesitation. My eyes rolled back into my head at the accompanying sensation of the plug massaging my channel and stretching me.

My cock bucked and drips of pre-cum fell between my legs and onto the floor, heedless of the pain that came from the burn.

The torment continued when Bailey pressed against my other side and I realised he'd got down on his knees. I glanced towards him, begging with my eyes that he kiss me. He glanced up at Jake silently and must have received approval because the next thing, he was devouring my mouth.

His tongue stroked against mine, and the taste of him on my lips, with the feel of the plug in my arse, left me close to the edge. I moaned in delight as Jake nudged the plug in my backside.

"Such a needy pup," he growled, sounding more animalistic than me.

A warm hand stroked over my arse. Who was touching me? The rough callus on the palm said it was Bailey and I groaned anew as he ran his fingers around where the plug was seated in my arse. The joint-teasing too much and I arched, my balls aching with the need to come.

However, a hand quickly took hold of my balls in a punishing grip.

"Arghhhhh," I cried into Bailey's mouth, making him chuckle as he moved back.

"You're not allowed to come, Pup. As we know, you have a little problem with control,

I'll strap up your balls to give you a helping hand," Jake rasped.

I moaned in complaint as, good to his word, Jake trussed up my balls, forcing my cock to protrude further from my body. He admired his handiwork before he slapped my arse. There was a flash of heat from the stinging blow that set off tiny fires in my arse cheek.

"Let's play." Jake sounded so genuinely happy that I ignored the tight feeling constricting my sac and chased after the ball he threw to the other side of the room.

His laughter was joined by Bailey's as I yipped and raced around the open floor space chasing the ball. The feeling of freedom came fast, and I lost myself in the pleasure of letting go of all my worries. My mind emptied while I skidded over the wooden floor, using my left leg as a sort of break to help me stay balanced. I returned to Jake and Bailey time and time again. They were both sitting on the sofa, each taking turns to throw the ball for me.

For what felt like the fiftieth time, with the ball clenched between my teeth, I returned to a grinning Jake. "Drop it, Pup."

His fingers came up and I shook my head and snarled at him playfully. A dark desire replaced the humour in his eyes and his fingers tugged on the ball again. "Are you being a disobedient pup?"

I shook my head, still not releasing the ball. He tutted and looked at Bailey. "Sit back, sub. I think Pup needs to be taught how to behave like a good puppy." His voice was laced with desire, and I shivered in anticipation.

Bailey's cock jerked as he shifted back until he pressed against the cushions and then sat waiting for whatever Jake was going to insist he do next. His face was a composed mask, but I could see the nerves in his twitching limbs. I wasn't much better.

My heart lodged itself in my throat when Jake spoke next. "Do you have condoms in your bag, Pup?"

Condoms? Plural?

I nodded and looked at Bailey, who sat with a wide-eyed expression. Jake couldn't fuck Bailey if he were sitting, so why did we need more than one condom?

The visual that popped into my head got me squeezing my butt cheeks, and I groaned as that caused the plug to give my prostate a nice nudge.

"Enjoying yourself, Pup?" Jake's brow rose as he moved back towards us, holding the lube bottle and two condoms. Oh fuck, would I be able to cope with both of them in my body? I had some pretty thick dildos I'd used in the past and yeah, they'd felt good, but two dicks crammed in my arse? Not so sure about that.

"Do you need to safe word, Sam?"

The question filtered past my worry, and I considered I'd maybe projected my thoughts a little loudly. Did I want to safe word? I waited to register my gut reaction, which was a 'hell no', as my brain caught up. *I can safe word any time, and Jake will stop.* As the truth of that registered, I looked at him and shook my head, barking.

His body visibly relaxed as a feral grin formed on his face. "I'll help you up onto the sofa."

What he actually meant was he'd lift me bodily off the floor. His muscles flexed and bunched under my weight, and Bailey moaned as Jake positioned me to straddle his lap. The deep cushions helped to support my knees.

Face to face with Bailey, I didn't think twice as I moved forward to kiss him. I swept my tongue over his mouth, encouraging him to open. Jake murmured next to my ear, "So fucking hot," and Bailey opened to me.

His tongue slid against mine, and then Jake's mouth joined in the fun. His lips pressed to the side of mine and Bailey's right before he slipped his tongue between us and we both sucked on it. It was messy, and the sexiest kiss I'd ever experienced. There were so many moans, groans, and whimpers, I wasn't sure who they were coming from as Jake dominated both Bailey and me.

Chapter Eighteen

Jake

The need for air won out, so I reluctantly released their mouths when the burn in my lungs became too much. My chest was heaving, and I couldn't seem to get my brain to function, to pull in enough air to fix the problem. It didn't help when I looked down at the tail in Sam's arse and thought about what was coming next.

When I felt able to be gentle, I carefully tugged the plug out and replaced it with my fingers I'd lubed before I'd had the need to join in the kiss. Sam's breath caught, and he made a mewling sound as I sunk three fingers into his relaxed hole. The plug had helped to relax the tight ring of muscle, but it was still a squeeze.

Sam made a growly noise, his hips tilting. The action spoke for him, so I plunged a little deeper to give him what he wanted. The burn, I'd bet, was delicious the way he ground back against me, asking for yet more. He seemed to lose himself in his pleasure and started to hump Bailey, much like a dog in heat. Then Sam lifted his bottom higher, invitingly.

The tight hold on my control slipped a little, and I had to take a deep breath and shut out the sounds and scent of arousal to stop myself mounting Sam before he was ready.

Several breaths later and with Sam whining, I replaced my three fingers with four and his channel convulsed. He quickly shut up as his silky channel continued to ripple and the seconds stretched as I waited for him to relax. It was only when he went back to rutting against Bailey, who was starting to look a little desperate as he stared over Sam's shoulder, his eyes begging me to hurry, that I moved my fingers.

With Bailey's begging eyes doing a number on me, Sam then lay his head on Bailey's shoulder. His half-masked face didn't shield what he was feeling, and he looked at me with the same adoration that Bailey wore.

I was screwed, well and fucking truly!

I wasn't sure if either man realised how they were staring at me, but they left me struggling to concentrate with so many emotions consuming me. To be the centre of their attention was like nothing before, it was everything I'd ever wanted. The throbbing in the centre of my chest was only surpassed by the growing need to claim these men as mine in the most primal way.

Sweat coated my skin by the time I deemed Sam ready. I hoped I'd done enough as I made quick work of putting a condom on me and then Bailey. He hissed at my touch, and if I'd not been desperate myself to sink into Sam and feel Bailey's cock pulse against mine, I'd have teased him further.

Sam seemed lost in his own little world when I encouraged his hips to lift so he could sink down onto Bailey's cock.

His eyelashes fluttered behind the mask as his head moved restlessly on Bailey's broad shoulder. "Oh, Bailey," he cried as I guided him onto Bailey's cock.

Once Bailey was seated inside Sam, I kept hold of his hips and moved to push the tip of my cock against the rim of his already full arse. "Relax, Pup," I ground out through clenched teeth as my jaw bunched at the strain of keeping control while the heat of his channel penetrated the latex and I pushed the head of my cock into his straining body.

Motherfuckingbastard!

I was sure my eyes crossed as indescribable pleasure and pain rocketed through me and pulsed at my very core. *These men are mine!* It roared inside my head, adding to the overwhelming sensations that left me speechless.

I swallowed hard enough to hear it ring in my ears.

Both men seemed to vibrate as one as they appeared to hold their collective breaths as I claimed them both as mine. They held each other but their eyes were firmly fixed on me, and my heart soared from the beauty of the moment. "So beautiful. So goddamn beautiful. Look at you both," I rasped in a tight voice that was full of everything I felt right then.

"Please...don't...talk," Sam panted, his body seemingly unsure if he wanted this as his arse clenched down painfully on my cock, crushing it against Bailey's. We both groaned in unison as Sam released then did it again. "Oh fuckkkkkkk...the...burnnnn...is incredible," Sam cried out, and started to rock.

I choked on my strangled chuckle as I gasped and slid deeper into the most incredible heat. Bailey's cock slid against mine and Sam didn't give me a second to adjust as he went wild, rocking back and forth. His body was slick with sweat as he mewled, lifting his hips to thrust back and down.

"No...fucker...move," Bailey rasped, not many seconds later. Utter desperation shone from his strained expression. "Can I come, Sir?" he pleaded.

"Yes." The word had barely left my dry lips when Sam did the squeezing thing again. The walls of his channel convulsed while he rocked down and back. Bailey's cock seemed to swell further, and Sam jerked and screamed as my own cock convulsed and shot pulse after pulse of cum inside Sam.

"My balls, oh fuck," Sam whined, his body pushing against Bailey as if seeking to come.

The orgasm made it hard to think. Then Bailey shifted and his hand disappeared, and I cursed that I'd not released the strapping. Seconds later, Sam gave a guttural cry and collapsed back against me. His slick back stuck to my sweat drenched chest. His head lolled on my shoulder as he shivered and shuddered for a long minute.

I met Bailey's gaze and a lazy smile spread over his lips. "I think we might have worn Pup out."

"I think you might be right," I replied, grinning back at him.

Sam snorted indignantly but didn't contradict us as his chest rose and fell in quick succession and he released a long sigh of contentedness.

Chapter Nineteen

*B*ailey

Humming to myself, I listened to Aaron Smith as I moved around the living room, dusting. Parts of my body ached and reminded me yet again how inventive Jake was as a Dom. Ever since he'd caught me and Sam in the playroom two months ago, he seemed to make it his mission to find new ways to show Sam and me how much he wanted us. And if that involved punishment for any kind of infraction he deemed we'd committed, then who was I to complain.

What I'd quickly discovered was that Sam liked to rebel and loved to get me into hot water with Jake and then help him torment me until I begged for mercy. *And you love it, so stop your moaning.*

Convinced I wore a sappy grin, I shook my head and sighed as I sprayed the top of the wooden cabinet that housed some of Jake's possessions. The scent of furniture polish distracted me, and I sneezed while I rubbed at the dusty wood.

It had been a couple of weeks since I'd last done it. When I spent my time focused on my two men to make sure they were happy, it often left me playing catch up. Not that either man complained about a little dust. It's just that I liked to make sure everything was perfect for them and make their lives a little easier.

I'd started to see myself a little like the stay-at-home husband...and I was okay with that. If I secretly hoped we'd move things to that stage at some point, then it wasn't harming anyone. Jake had declared his feelings, and every day I expected Sam to declare his too. I'd accepted how I felt for both men, but I was nervous about coming right out and saying it after the disaster with Sam. I didn't want him feeling hurt at my easy acceptance of the love I felt for Jake when he'd struggled to get me to admit my love for him. So I'd kept silent, hoping to find the right moment.

It was getting harder and harder not to express myself. Jake showed how much he relished the role I'd embraced like no other. My whole life, I'd never allowed the inner me to just let go and be myself but living with Jake and Sam had changed that. They appreciated all the things I did for them and the praise I got from both men...

I cocked up my brow and eyed my shorts as my dick started to plump. My mind was only too happy to remind me of how both men showed their appreciation three nights earlier after I'd made them homemade pizza as a treat for dinner. They'd laid me on the bed after we'd eaten and had spent several hours tracing every muscle in my body with their tongues until I'd come.

"Stop right now," I muttered under my breath when my cock thickened further.

Years I'd been able to control my body's responses, with the army having given me the training ground. Only now, all I had to do was think about either man, and I got hard. This torment, I was sure, had everything to do with waking every damn day to Sam wrapped around me like a sweaty blanket and Jake touching me in some way. *This is not helping the cause!*

I huffed so loudly it drowned out the lyrics Aaron Smith was crooning for a few seconds. Tempted to shift my cock, I glanced warily towards the stairs, recalling the last time I touched my dick without permission. Jake had caught me red-handed, and I'd had to wear the dreaded cock cage while he'd positioned Sam on all fours and fucked him right in front of me.

I'd only been allowed to watch. It had been erotic torture of the best kind…well it would have been if not for the cock cage and the non-participation. Okay, it had been hell!

You have a safe word you could have used at any point, my inner voice stated in a snarky tone, not letting me get away with anything. Giving up my control to Jake was the best kind of aphrodisiac, and it gave me a sense of freedom I'd never experienced before with another Dom. Add to that Sam's mischievousness and exuberance, and I was in seventh heaven. *How is this my life?*

The throbbing ache that started to grow between my legs received several curses as I carried on dusting and pretended like nothing was happening in my nether regions. There was no way I was going to take any chances that Jake could return and catch me touching myself. Both men had plans that would require them to work long hours, so I was sure sex wasn't going to be on the agenda any time soon.

Jake had left for the office that morning unsure when he'd be back, with a new project giving him major headaches. He'd spoken about having to travel up north again, and I prayed he didn't have to.

Sam was going to be working for the next seven days straight as he'd taken over running both the Flamingo Bar and The Playroom. Ferron and Isaac were off to China and Nathan and Lenny were taking a few days now that the Flamingo Bar was running smoothly. They all needed some down time together after the court case three months earlier. Devon, a guy from Ferron's past, had been sentenced to four years in prison for kidnapping and beating up Lenny and Ferron. The fucker deserved more than that for what he'd done to Ferron alone.

I scrubbed at the top of the wood, trying to banish the image of Ferron's defeated face the first time I'd met him. The guy had shared some of his story, but the court case had revealed more. Nerves fluttered in my gut at recalling what I'd read in the papers.

My knuckles turned white. There'd been whispers I'd heard that there was yet more to this story. The temptation to ask Ferron was dialed back when he seemed to be finding his feet and no longer looked as haunted as he had. He'd been a wreck over the court case and even more concerned for his lover, Isaac.

So, I'd let it be for the time being and promised myself I'd talk to Nathan about it when the time was right. I tried to keep my worry about any possible backlash, possibly even one that could strike at Sam while he worked at the club and bar, to myself. Granted, my concern wasn't only for Sam. Ferron worked in the same building and I loved the little guy.

Knowing how Isaac felt about him and that he'd been in the services, I'd wondered if he'd taken precautions to protect Ferron. The years in the army meant I could possibly help my friend. *Just ask Isaac the next time you see him.*

My phone buzzed on the table behind me and pulled me from my thoughts. When it continued to vibrate, I walked to it. Dropping the cloth and placing the can of polish on the table, I lifted the phone.

A smile spread over my face as I swiped at the screen, then pressed on the speaker icon. "I was thinking about you."

"Were you now? And what were you thinking about?" Jake asked, his voice dropping and deepening to a husky growl.

Where thoughts of Ferron had allowed my body to settle, Jake's question had the exact opposite effect. I gritted my teeth together to stop the moan from escaping. My heart thudded against my ribs as his breathing increased.

"You weren't misbehaving were you, sub?"

My palms grew sweaty at the longing that came from wanting to please my Dom. "I've been good, I swear, Sir."

"Then maybe I need to think about a reward. Would my sub like that?"

The moan was out this time before I could stop it, as my last reward popped into my head, something I was sure Jake had done deliberately.

"You want to feel my cock and Sam's stretching you, filling you till all you can feel is us?"

"Oh please...that...yes," I gasped and sweated, trying to resist touching the flagpole tenting my shorts. The epic tug of arousal in my lower abdomen tensed my stomach muscles.

There was an evil chuckle coming down the phone, and I sagged, knowing I wasn't going to like what was coming.

"You, my gorgeous sub, will have to wait, unfortunately." Jake's chuckles turned into a sigh when someone spoke in the background. "Hang on, Bai... Yes I am just sorting out the things I need to take with me."

He carried on talking to whoever was with him and my heart sank into my boots at what he was saying. The teasing tone in his voice was gone and he was all business. When he came back on the line, he sounded regretful. "Bai, can you pack a bag for me? Two suits, shirts, and underwear, my grooming kit should already be in my small carryon bag."

"How long are you going away for this time?" I asked as soon as he stopped talking. My ears were already buzzing from the thought of him being gone for days.

"Two days and possibly two nights. I'm flying out of Heathrow in four hours, hence the call as it doesn't leave me time to drive home, pack, and get to the airport if I account for murderous traffic at this time of the day. I'm sorry, Bai, you know how much I hate to leave you both."

There was emotion in his voice that caused my heart to flutter madly. "It's fine. I'll pack your bag. I'll be waiting at the door for you if you let me know what time you'll be here. Have you told Sam?" Sadness replaced my excited buzz, knowing how upset Sam would be.

We'd both come to hate the times Jake had to go away. Although it had only been a handful of trips, most of which were only overnight, we'd still missed him. Sam had grown used to having Jake spoon him when he went to sleep. Initially I'd been a little jealous that Sam wasn't satisfied with just me, until I'd also found myself mooning over Jake not being with us.

A dejected sigh escaped as Jake spoke. "No, he was going to be my next call."

"I'll do it, Sir, and save you from the fifty questions Sammy will fire at you," I offered, trying to inject a lightness I didn't feel.

"Thank you, Bai. I'll message you when I'm near the house." With a quick goodbye the call ended.

I sucked in a deep breath, preparing myself for an upset Sam as I searched for his number and hit dial. One thing I hated more than upsetting my Dom, was upsetting Sammy. *You can console him when he comes home. Yeah, like that will work without Jake!*

"Yo, Bailey, everything okay?"

Chapter Twenty

Sam

Bailey tucked me into his body as we sat on the sofa waiting for Jake to FaceTime. It had been two days since he'd left, and both of us were missing him. Work for him and me was turning into a nightmare, but I'd kept silent.

The ringing iPad pulled me from my thoughts as Bailey clicked to connect and Jake's smiling face appeared on the screen. "Oh, look at my guys. I wish I were cuddled up there between you both." His voice sounded tired and there was strain about his eyes.

"How are things going?" I questioned as Bailey stroked my hair.

"Let's not talk about my work. What have you too been up to? Are you missing me yet?"

Bailey chuckled. "I've a new spot in the bed because someone can't sleep without being spooned."

"Hey, is it my fault you two have spoiled me?" I complained good-naturedly as Jake grinned at us.

"I'm pleased to hear you're missing your big spoon."

I rolled my eyes as Bailey continued to chuckle. "I think I'm actually the big spoon. I

mean look at the size of me next to you two."
His cheekiness was something he didn't often
let out, but I loved it when Bailey was like this.

"Are you looking for a punishment when I
get back?" Jake's voice deepened, and Bailey's
body responded as my bottom ground down
on the plumping cock beneath me.

"He is—"

Bailey covered my mouth with his hand,
and I licked his palm. "Yuck, stop licking me,"
he complained.

"Then don't cover my mouth," I answered
back, causing Jake to laugh at our antics. It was
a great sound and the feelings of longing for
him receded a little. It was always harder on
me, somehow, when Jake had to go on one of
his trips.

We carried on chatting for another hour
before Jake started to yawn. After the call
ended, I curled up on Bailey and sighed. "I wish
Jake didn't have to go away."

"Me, too. Me too." Bailey lowered his chin
to the top of my head, and he gave an
answering sigh as we stared at the muted TV.

The week seemed endless already, and I
still had five more long days at work, on top of
Jake being away. I snuggled into Bailey's arms
and drew his scent in as he held me tighter.

"He'll be back before you know it," Bailey
promised.

Four days later I was glad Jake wasn't home, even though I was missing him terribly. It took all my effort to keep quiet as I moved around in the master bathroom after I'd snuck past a sleeping Bailey. I didn't want him to wake and catch me when I couldn't hide the pain that was whipping my arse better than Jake could. I filled the bath and kept a watchful eye on the door as I sat on the edge of the tub and stripped off my clothes. My lips trembled as I looked down at my stump with tear drenched eyes that blurred my vision.

Day six of working twelve-hour days, and my body had had enough. Tears dripped off my chin as I eased my throbbing leg into the hot water. I hissed through my teeth as the water lapped at the raw skin on my stump. My stump was so painful, I could barely touch it, never mind tolerate my prosthetic limb rubbing against the inflamed flesh.

When I'd agreed to help cover both bar and club, I'd not given any thought to how much walking I'd have to do, particularly between the two floors. The lift was often full of patrons, so I'd habitually taken to the stairs which was quicker, though definitely the more unforgiving option. I'd lost count of how many times I'd been up and down them over the last six days. My physio would be proud. *Would he really?*

Ignoring the question, I sank back into the full tub of steaming hot water and prayed it would help ease the deep ache that seemed to have spread throughout my whole body tonight. The scent of Epsom salts wafted up on the steam as I shut my blurry eyes. Tears continued to rain down my face as I quietly sobbed.

I'd been careful not to let on to Bailey how bad I was suffering, for fear he'd tell Jake. Between the two of them, they were like a pair of mother hens at times. And most of the time I loved it, but when my leg was involved, I sometimes struggled to see it as well-meaning.

You mean you think that they'll see you as less!

The sneak attack by my ego added to my woes as I couldn't deny that was exactly how I felt when there was nothing but pain and frustration at my own lack.

Hot water lapped at my body as I floated in the tub and let the pills I'd dry swallowed in the cab home cloud my mind and worrisome thoughts. Something I'd been doing increasingly over the last two days to just get through. I hated living on painkillers, but there was little else I could do with my schedule. *Only one more day.*

I focused on that and prayed for the strength I'd need to get through the following day before I had five days off. My plan for them was to find a flat surface, preferably Jake's bed, with him and Bailey cocooning me.

If Jake gets home!

A tremulous hiccup was followed by another sob when a wave of despondency rolled over me. Jake's trip away had gone from four days to seven, but he was allegedly due home the next day. *If there are no other disasters to befall the project.*

I sagged into the water and kept my eyes shut, working to block out the whiny voice.

Jake hadn't gone into great detail, but it seemed the contractor in charge of implementing Jake's designs had cut a few corners. That had resulted in one of the main walls collapsing and killing one man and injuring another.

The fucker of a contractor had then tried to say it was a design flaw that had caused the incident. It had taken four days to unravel the mess to discover the substandard supplies the firm had used had been the cause. Jake had been devastated, and it left a nasty ache in my chest that neither me nor Bailey could do a thing to comfort him while he was so far away.

The FaceTime calls between us all helped, but it was why I'd also driven myself into the ground at work. I'd needed something to vent my frustration out on. Bailey, on the other hand, had vented his on the house, which positively gleamed. The windows and every surface shone like a new pin. I'd swear you could eat a meal off the floors.

"Oh, baby, what is it?" I jerked my eyes open at the sound of Bailey's cry.

I'd been so lost in my misery, I'd never heard him enter the bathroom. His face was a picture of despair as he sank next to the bath.

The tears refused to stop as I sobbed, "I'm in so much pain."

He immediately got off the floor and stripped off his sleep pants. "Sit forward, Sammy, let me get in behind you."

The bathtub was huge and could easily fit two men of our size, so I didn't hesitate. He got in behind me and sat, the water level creeping to within inches of the top of the bath. His legs stretched down the side of my body, careful not to knock me.

"Lie back against my chest," he crooned softly in my ear.

Too tired to do more than he asked, I rested back against his broad, solid chest. The beat of his heart comforted me as he soaped his large hands, then moved them up to my shoulders. His fingers dug into the tight muscles, and he worked to release the knots. He stroked from my shoulders, down my chest. Stopping at my waistline, he moved to my arms next. By the time he'd got to the fingers on my left arm, I was floating in a pleasurable haze. The pain in my stump was still there, but it had scaled back from a solid ten to a more manageable five.

He shifted me a little so his hands could massage up and down my thighs. His fingers were pure magic and my eyes drifted closed.

Unaware of how long we stayed like that, I tried to lift my eyelids when Bailey whispered in my ear, "I'm going to get out now, and I'll be back in a minute to get you."

Too tired to protest, I let him move me so he could slip out of the bath. I drifted in a sleepy haze until I felt arms slide under my back and legs. My tongue felt too thick as I tried to form a protest as I was lifted straight out of the bath.

A fluttering started in my chest as it registered the show of brute strength. I was by no means small, but Bailey lifted me as if I weighed nothing. My sluggish mind tried to compute why he wasn't putting me down so I could hop to the bedroom. Not that I was at all sure I had the strength, but I could try.

The feel of a towel against my wet flesh registered past the tired haze. With the drugs and weariness, I couldn't figure out how the towel had got onto the bed, so I gave up trying. I curled into a ball and snuggled into the Lenor-scented fabric.

The sound of a chuckle was the last thing I heard as sleep dragged me into the darkness and away from the pain.

***

Something soft stroked my cheek, and I pried open my bleary eyes, a smile quickly spreading over my face. The wave of emotions at seeing Jake bent over me were too much to contain as I reached up to wrap my arms around his neck. The need to kiss him fought and won over any worry about my morning breath.

"I've missed you," I whispered against his plump lips, right before he gave me the sweetest kiss. It went on and on until my chest felt like it would burst from the lack of oxygen. I chuckled breathlessly as I pulled back and saw the look of disappointment on Jake's face. "I need to breathe."

A beautiful smile warmed his eyes. "That you do, especially for what I've planned. I've missed you, sweet Pup, and...where's Bai?" His gaze moved over the bed and the brightness of his smile dimmed a little. "He wasn't upstairs, I checked before I came here." His brow furrowed as I glanced over my shoulder at the empty bed and my stomach took a nosedive.

Whenever Jake went away, Bailey always lay behind me to spoon me as I found it easier to sleep. I tried to recall what had happened after Bailey had got in the bath with me. Did I dream of him carrying me and laying me on the bed? My stump gave me a sharp reminder as I shifted, and it woke up.

"Oh, Sir, you're home," Bailey all but sang with joy as he entered the room, a bag clutched in one hand that looked suspiciously like a pharmacy bag. His face was flushed, and he was dressed for cooler weather. September so far had been rather chilly.

Oh shit! I eyed both men warily, my stomach now deciding to do an acrobatic display for me, making me grateful I'd not eaten or drank in hours. Would Bailey rat me out?

"Where have you been?" Jake asked as he opened his arms when Bailey approached hurriedly.

I held my breath and prayed to the gods.

"I went out to the pharmacy around the corner to see what they had to help with the raw skin on Sammy's stump," he said in an excited rush as Jake cuddled him.

I deflated quicker than a bloody balloon. I couldn't see Jake's face, but I could easily read the sudden tension in his body. It was enough to alert me that he was upset by Bailey's remarks.

"It's fine this morning. I was just a little sore last night." The whine in my voice was embarrassing.

Bailey twisted to look at me and one dark brow arched and made me believe Elvis Presley would have been envious of the move. With nowhere to hide from the heat that rode up my chest and into my face, I shifted uncomfortably on the bed.

Jake glanced between me and Bailey. "What's going on here?" Jake held up his finger, stopping me dead in my tracks. The lie that was on the tip of my tongue shrivelled up and died while I struggled to hold his stare. "I want the truth, Pup," he growled low in his throat.

My cock, clearly a sadistic fool, plumped, and I cast a wary look at Bailey, who remained silent but with a glint of steel in his eyes that said he wasn't going to cover for me.

I sagged against the mattress. "All right. You pair need a warning label. Beware, they'll gang up on you when you least expect it," I complained, albeit half-heartedly. Secretly I was pleased that they cared about my well-being, when so few had done so in the past. Warmth filled my chest, only this time it wasn't from embarrassment.

Silence was a deadly weapon when both men used it together. I licked my dry lips and tried to find a way to respond without dropping myself in any more hot water.

Chapter Twenty-One

Jake

As soon as I'd known I could fly home last night, I'd rearranged my flight for this morning so I could return from Edinburgh on the first flight back to London. I'd arrived in London just after seven-thirty a.m. and I'd been able to fight through the traffic and arrive home in less than two hours.

On the way home, I'd called the office to tell them I'd not be in today or for the rest of the week. I needed my men after last week. It was all I could think about, having them both wrapped in my arms, naked and in bed.

What I'd not expected to find was Sam sleeping like the dead with dark circles around his eyes and looking gaunt. The second surprise was to find Bailey not in bed with Sam. He was the early riser out of the three of us, the army too ingrained, he'd said, to change his habits. But with me away, I'd expected him to be tucked up around Sam. He'd confessed he missed me terribly, and although he loved to wrap around Bailey, Sam always felt more secure when I was away with Bailey spooning him.

It was one of the many things I'd learned over the last few months as we'd established our own routine and habits that left me in no doubt about the love I felt for both men. I was firmly attached, and now couldn't envision my life without either man. Bailey was by far the easier to live with as he loved being submissive, whereas Sam was a submissive when it suited him. His preference, on the whole, was for me to be in control, with one exception, his leg. He liked to push himself and didn't seem to understand that it hurt my heart when he was in pain or struggling.

I eyed the mutinous scowl that was now forming and didn't disguise the pain he was in. The dark circles and gaunt expression were now making more sense. He'd clearly overdone things while I'd been away.

"Work's as much of a bastard as yours has been. My stump is a little raw from the amount of activity it's seen over the last few days. That's all," Sam replied as I remained silent next to Bailey.

I arched my brow, much as Bailey had, and stared Sam down. "Is that all? Show me your stump and I'll be the judge of that."

Bailey remained rooted to the spot as I walked to the bed and Sam clutched at the patterned duvet cover, his eyes glowing with defiance.

Seeing I was going to have a battle on my hands, I deepened my voice, knowing the effect it would have on him. "I won't ask again. Show me your leg."

The predictable flare of arousal in his gaze was quickly followed by his eyes narrowing. "You did that on purpose. I told you, my leg is fine." He glanced over to Bailey. "Bailey is just over-reacting is all."

His voice lacked conviction and Bailey coughed, though I wasn't sure if it was from distress or hiding his amusement as I kept my gaze on Sam.

"Are you safe wording?"

Sam's eyes widened with alarm and his head shook. "No."

At his response, I whisked the duvet up from the bottom of the bed and threw it to the side to reveal Sam's lower body. Sam seemed to freeze in place as I glanced at his right leg and winced at the dark-red, swollen stump. A tight band of pain encircled my chest thinking about how he must be hurting.

I met his sullen expression with one of angry frustration. "I'm disappointed that you chose to lie to me. Right now, my only concern is ensuring we find a way to ease the swelling and find something that will help with the raw, inflamed skin. That will hopefully help with the pain you must be in." I took a deep breath to control my temper. "But when you're fully healed, we are going to talk about a punishment suitable for your actions."

The disappointment in my voice was clear to hear and Sam's head dropped. His gaze on the bed, he didn't argue back. Bailey stepped closer to me, as if seeking to comfort me, while his gaze went to Sam.

Recalling the bag Bailey held, I asked, "What did you manage to find at the chemist?"

"They suggested Sudocrem for the raw skin. I got these large thick pads that will cushion his knee—"

"Isn't that for like, nappy rash? And I can't use those pads because my prosthetic is moulded to my stump. I've coverings that fit, a thick pad won't work," Sam advised, sounding more than a little pissed-off as he made no effort to look at either me or Bailey.

Bailey carried on like Sam hadn't interrupted him. "I got ice packs and a heat pack. The guy behind the counter said to alternate between the two to reduce the swelling."

I laid my hand on Bailey's arm, making him look at me. I gave him a warm smile. "Thank you, Bai, that was very thoughtful. Will you please take the ice packs and pop them in the freezer and warm the heat pad for me?"

His face brightened and he took the things he needed out of the bag, offering me the remaining items. Once he'd left the room, I moved my gaze back to the man sat with slumped shoulders, plucking at the part of the duvet still covering his waist.

"You can stop this nonsense right now. You've hurt yourself and I won't tolerate that. We'll put on a warm pack, then a cold one, before I put some cream over the raw skin. You'll need to leave your prosthetic limb off today—"

"What! I'm not going to be able to get about with my crutches behind the bar, are you mad?" he snarled indignantly, meeting my angry glare.

"Oh, you're clearly in the mood to push your luck right now," I growled.

"I've got to work, it's as simple as that"— his gaze moved to the small clock sat on the bedside table before he looked back at me— "in three hours. I'm the manager of the club and bar this week. I assured Nathan I could manage, and I have."

The message was loud and very clear, he wasn't going to listen to what I said even when his leg clearly showed that he was physically struggling.

"I've no doubt in my mind that you are more than capable of running both. You're a bright man with so much energy. However, that being said, you have to consider your physical limitations."

"Dreamcatcher!"

I bit my lip hard enough to taste blood at hearing him say his safe word. My lip throbbed painfully and matched the ache developing in my chest. I masked the hurt and blanked my expression as I met his defiant eyes. I nodded resignedly. "Okay, I'll leave you to it."

I spun around before I could start to beg him to listen to reason and stalked out of the room, honouring his decision to safe word. For the first time in my life, I cursed the lifestyle I'd chosen to live when all I wanted to do was wrap Sam in my arms and protect him from more pain and suffering.

He doesn't want it from you, he safe worded!

Oh, fuck off!

Chapter Twenty-Two

Bailey

I'd been so happy to have Jake home that it was only when I went up to the kitchen that I realised I might have caused a problem for Sam. I shook off the worry and placed the ice packs in the freezer before reading the instructions on the heat pack.

When the pack was hot, I wrapped it in a small piece of an old T-shirt I'd cut for dust rags that I hadn't used yet. I was about to head back down the stairs when Jake appeared. My pulse started to pound as I took in his dejected expression and sad eyes.

"What happened, Sir?" I asked in a whisper, frightened to hear the answer when deep down I knew Sam had rebelled against Jake's dominance. It wasn't uncommon when it came to Sam's need to show he could match anyone without a disability. No matter how many times we'd tried to show him and tell him that he was an equal match for any person, he pushed like he'd done this last week until his body couldn't take anymore.

"Sam safe worded when I mentioned his physical limitations. But damn it, he needs to think about the damage he's causing to his leg. He isn't fit to go to work and stand for however many hours with his leg that swollen and inflamed. He'll put that damn prosthetic leg on, knowing it will hurt him," Jake ground out through clenched teeth as he ran his hands through his already ruffled hair. His whole body seemed to quiver when he stalked past me to go and stare out of the window that overlooked part of the London skyline.

The warmth of the pad drew my attention and I sighed. "Should I give him the heat pad?"

"I'm sure he'll need it"—he shrugged and continued to stare out of the window, his stance stiff—"but whether he'll accept it is another matter."

His voice was flat and lacked any of the emotion from moments earlier. This happened when he closed in on himself. He didn't do it often. It was only, I'd noticed, when there was friction between any of us and he needed time to figure out what to do. Jake was a fixer and hated when he couldn't make things work for all of us.

I wanted to reach out to him, to go and kneel at his side, but with Sam in pain, I ignored my own needs. "I'll go and see if I can talk some sense into him," I offered, but my gut tightened.

"Thank you, Bai. I wasn't going to go into work today, or the rest of the week, but I've changed my mind. I'm not sure I can watch him leave, knowing he's going to hurt himself by being a stubborn-headed fool."

His tone left me feeling tearful and fretful. Would he decide we were too much trouble? I didn't often have these thoughts, but sometimes, when Sam pushed too hard, it did make me wonder if there was a tipping point with so many emotions involved.

An urge to puke all over the floor took hold and choked me as the idea wouldn't let go this time around. I swallowed the bile burning my oesophagus and coughed to clear my throat. "Whatever you think is best." My voice shook, but he didn't turn to look at me, so I quickly left before I burst into tears and begged him not to go.

I was breathing hard and struggling to contain my emotions as I entered the bedroom to find Sam sat where I'd left him. He was quietly sobbing, his head buried in his hands. As much as I wanted to be angry with him for being pig-headed, my heart ached for the man who'd endured so much. So instead of pointing out the obvious, I ran across the room and crawled onto the bed to sit next to him.

He looked up, and his puffy, red-rimmed eyes pleaded with me. "I...I upset Jake," he sobbed as fresh tears fell in big droplets down the side of his cheeks. "Did he leave? Please say he didn't leave," he asked anxiously.

"He's leaving to go into the office…today," I replied, unable to mask my own fears.

"Oh…he must be mad," Sam whispered, his chin trembling. "Did he tell you what I did?"

I nodded and dropped my gaze to Sam's uncovered stump. "I should put this heat pack on if you're going to work. You'll need to swap it out for the ice pack a few times until you have to leave. Hopefully, it'll help." I opted to keep my own thoughts to myself at how I thought it would make little difference once he put his leg on.

He gave a resigned sigh. "I have to go, it's my bloody job. He has to travel and go to places, like Scotland, and I don't want him to go. But I don't beg like I want to, to get him to stay, because I know he has to go to work. Why can't he see it's the same for me? I know I have a disability,"—he poked at his stump, scowling—"it's not like I can forget."

When he stopped for a moment and returned his gaze to mine, I choked back a ball of emotion. The rawness in the depth of his gaze was gutting. The fear of rejection was there, and it stole my breath more effectively than being submerged in water. I struggled to hold his gaze as he started to talk and lay himself bare.

"My whole life I've had to take care of myself. Look out for myself because no one else has ever cared enough to stay. Not once…you hear me? Not once!" he cried in anguish.

His eyes were back to brimming with tears and I quickly wrapped my arm around his back and encouraged him to lean on me. "You're not alone anymore, baby. I swear to you, I'm going nowhere." I pushed my fear aside at the realisation I'd fight tooth and nail to keep what we all had together.

Sam was mine as much as Jake, we were all a unit. Sam needed Jake as much as I did. These past few months had shown me that. Jake was a vital part to both our lives, and as I wiped at Sam's face and got him to look at me, I hoped against hope I wasn't setting us both up for a fall.

"You have me, *and Jake,* and we want to take care of you. We love you and you have nothing to prove to either of us." I hoped I was reading his fears right as I stroked at his quivering cheeks. "All those people in the past didn't see how wonderful you are, but we do."

"He's right, we do," came Jake's deep voice from the doorway.

Sam jerked against me before he looked towards Jake.

Had Jake heard all of the conversation? I glanced at him from under my eyelashes and heat filled my face at the look of love Jake revealed as he stared at us both.

He stepped closer to the bed, his hands shoved into his suit trouser pockets. His tie sat askew, and his hair was a mess. For the first time since I'd met him, there was an air of uncertainty about him and he didn't look as put together as he normally did.

"All those months ago, when Nathan suggested to me that you pair might give me what was missing from my life, I never dreamed this is where it would lead. You two are the best thing that has ever happened to me. I love you both in equal measures. You are both what's most important in my life. Sometimes, I can't see past that."

Jake looked directly at Sam and then down at his right leg. "Your disability doesn't make you any less than anybody else in my eyes. If anything, it shows me how lucky I am to have someone who has endured so much and come through stronger and more determined to succeed."

What about me? All I'd shown was what a coward I was. As if Jake had read my mind, he turned his attention to me and the air in the room disappeared.

"You've always put Sam's needs first. You might not think of it like that, but I do. You couldn't give him what he wanted or what he needed. The strength it took to step back from love in the hope that the other person can find it with someone else is not cowardice. Fuck, in my eyes it shows your true courage and strength." His voice was full of conviction.

A smile formed on Sam's face as he drew my attention by nudging my ribs with his elbow. "He's right, you know? It might have taken me a while to figure it out, but you have always put me first. I love you." Sam shifted his gaze to Jake. "I love you, and I'm sorry for getting cross earlier...I was scared that..." he shrugged, his chin dipping.

"That I might not want someone who's not perfect?" Jake filled in, and Sam nodded, still not meeting Jake's gaze. "Well I hate to break it to you, Sam, but I figured that out a long time ago. You are pushy, mischievous, and more often than not an exuberant pup, and I wouldn't change that for the world."

Jake chuckled as Sam's head came up quick-smart and he snorted.

"No one is perfect, Sammy, no one. But you and Bailey are perfect to me and *for* me."

His voice thickened, and I shifted on the bed as I realised what I was about to do. "I love you." I echoed the sentiments of the other men, knowing it to be the truth. I'd never thought I'd have enough room to love more than one man, Sam, but Jake had proved me wrong.

Jake made a dive onto the side of the bed I was sat on. I grinned, knowing it was to avoid Sam's legs. He had a big grin on his face as he moved so he could wrap his arms around Sam and me. I snuggled into his sweet-smelling embrace with Sam crushed between us both.

"Now we have the love confessions out of the way, how do we overcome the little issue from earlier, Pup?" Jake asked, making Sam groan, and me laugh.

You have to love a Dom for their tenacity!

Chapter Twenty-Three

Sam

A scowl formed on my face, I could feel it, but there was nothing I could do about it as I eyed my two new members of staff for the day. I pretended I didn't feel the excited flutter in my chest or the proceeding warmth that accompanied it. *They'd come to help! They'd come to help me get through the day!*

I blinked rapidly and looked back down at the computer sat in front of me, that I'd opened but hadn't done a stroke of work on. The spreadsheet figures blurred into a big black blob as I repeatedly swallowed. The noise in the room faded into the background.

When Jake had brought up me working today after...what had he called it? *Our love fest.* Yeah, it had been that. What else could it be called when we'd all declared our feelings for the first time to each other? It had been a beautiful moment and I'd wanted to revel in it. *No, you wanted to avoid what had started the love fest!*

I stooped over the computer and hoped neither man was watching me too closely. Jake, being the Dom he was, wouldn't let me avoid what had started the conversation in the first place and had suggested something so bizarre I'd thought he'd been joking.

I recalled his deadly serious face when he'd explained his plan for *my* day.

"I was thinking downstairs, which is why I came up to talk to you both before our love fest." Jake stroked a hand down my back, distracting me from what he was saying.

"Bailey and I will spend the day with you, and we can do the running around for you. That way you can leave off your prosthetic."

What did he just say? *I pulled back, giving myself some breathing room. Bailey sat cuddled into my side, unmoving. Had he said they'd come to work with me? I must have heard wrong. Clearly it was a ridiculous suggestion. I mean he had to be kidding. They couldn't just spend the day running around after me, or for me. No one offered to do that.*

I eyed Jake, and the serious look on his face was enough for me to huff out a breath of confusion. My fringe lifted and dropped into my eyes. I brushed it out of the way and gave Jake what I hoped wasn't the grimace I felt at thoughts of him bossing me around in front of my work colleagues. I might love him doing that at home, but there was no way I wanted him doing it at work. "I'm not sure that's a good idea, Jake."

"Why? It's the perfect solution. We get to spend the day together, and we can lighten the

load for you. You'll have less pain and discomfort. What's not good about that?" His brows rose, a look of expectation on his face.

I was sure I could come up with several reasons as to why it wasn't a good idea, but he looked so pleased with himself, I struggled to voice one. I caught Bailey's grin out of the side of my eye. The fucker knew I was doomed and wasn't going to rescue me.

I sagged and nodded. "All right...but don't forget I'm the boss, not you, when I'm at work."

I recalled those words as they ran through my head. *How's that working out for you, being the boss?*

I sighed in defeat and picked up my mug of lukewarm coffee, taking a drink to swallow the bitter taste in my mouth. Jake had, for his part, taken me at my word, and I hated being the boss! Okay, I didn't hate being the boss, just the boss of Jake when he'd got dressed for a day in a kink club and bar.

Had he dressed up as some sort of payback? My brows knitted together as I glanced down the busy bar to where he stood serving a customer. The leather trousers were bad enough. They were soft brown leather and clung to him in all the right places. The leather harness that revealed most of his chest left me achingly hard and distracted me from the pain in my stump. Leather wrapped seductively around his shoulders and his chest. There was a simple Celtic design crafted into the harness. His skin glowed against the brown leather and my mouth watered at the sight of his dark nipples.

"Do you want me to go down to The Playroom and grab the invoices from yesterday? You mentioned earlier they have to be inputted into the spreadsheet," Bailey asked, drawing my attention from Jake to him.

There was a gleam in his eyes that told me he knew exactly what I'd been thinking about. I eyed his outfit, which, in my opinion, was just as distracting as Jakes. In lieu of a leather harness, Bailey's broad chest was covered in a figure-hugging muscle shirt all in black. He might as well have been naked the way the T-shirt stuck to his rippling muscles. The black leather trousers weren't as fitted as Jake's, but they cupped his butt cheeks in the most delicious way, nevertheless.

Stop thinking about his butt!

Distractedly, I glanced away and looked about the busy bar. My lip curled into a back-off sneer as jealousy wormed its way into my gut. Several subs were making it obvious they were eyeing up Bailey. At first glance you'd definitely think Bailey was a Dom. His height and width and the way he carried himself spoke to the career he'd had in the army. It was only when you looked at his face and his posture that it became clear he was submissive. It was how he'd managed to fool me for all those years.

I laid my hand on his arm in a possessive gesture and met the gaze of those brave enough to continue to look our way.

Bailey's face morphed into a big grin. "You know I'm yours and Jake's."

The lack of prosthetic made believing that a little more difficult as I struggled to push the anxiety away, when what was lacking was more obvious. The confession from earlier had come out of the blue, in that I mean I'd had no intention of ever voicing those fears my past had created. But somehow, this morning's events had torn at my defence mechanisms and I'd been left exposed, apparently unable to keep my mouth shut.

One look at Jake's face when he'd come into the room and I'd known he'd heard my revelation. What had surprised me was that neither man seemed to see it as a weakness, this lack I had of being able to keep people wanting me for more than a short period of time.

Would this time really be different? Was the love between us enough?

"Wherever your head has just gone, stop right now. We love you, Sammy," Bailey growled, much like Jake liked to do, causing a shiver to run down my spine. Bailey reached across the bar and took the forgotten cup out of my hand and placed it down before he held both of my hands in his. "How do we prove to you that we love you and we're going nowhere?"

His earnest expression held a pleading quality that was difficult to ignore. "I'm not sure." Even as I said it, my eyes drifted to the unoccupied stage. The memory of the man displaying his puppy with pride filled my mind right along with the regret I'd never get the chance.

Bailey followed my gaze, looking over his shoulder, then he turned to face me again and his eyes had a calculating look in them. "Do you want to be mine and Jake's puppy here, in front of everyone?"

How had he guessed? *Erm hello, how do you think! More to the point, would you want to expose yourself in that way?* The inner self that remembered what it was like to be whole was desperate for the opportunity. The scared part that sometimes only saw what was left of my leg wasn't sure I was brave enough to ask for what I really wanted.

"How...I don't know?" I whispered fretfully, unsure how to respond.

"Listen, think about it. We love you and I'm sure I speak for Jake too when I say we'll do anything to show you that you're ours, now and forever."

There was confidence and a hint of the old Sarge in his voice, and I chuckled and nodded. "I'll think about it. But in the meantime, you need to get back to work. I thought you were going to go and get my invoices for me."

***

I'd taken Bailey's advice and thought about what would help alleviate my fear of losing them both. With the following days giving me lots of free time, and their insistence that I not so much as lift a finger, it had given me plenty of opportunity to mull over my past.

The other night at the bar, no one had so much as mentioned the crutches or my missing limb. In fact, from what I could tell, none of the staff had given me so much as a second glance and had treated me no differently. It got me thinking about what other misconceptions I had. It was a bitter pill to swallow, to realise that I had so many insecurities I'd not really faced.

The counselling I'd had post-surgery had been more focused on how to adapt to my new body and how I saw it. That didn't necessarily help when I'd so many insecurities from how I was treated as a child. My missing limb was only part of it, or more to the point, exacerbated what I'd hidden. A belief that I wasn't lovable.

Years of being rejected by one family after another, I'd learned to hide behind a happy-go-lucky façade, and that was hard to dig beneath. To poke at old wounds when they hurt and couldn't be changed, was hard. At three o'clock this morning, I'd faced the reality that I was punishing myself and my body for not being enough.

As I'd lain there, wrapped in Bailey's and Jake's loving embrace, I'd acknowledged that I needed to learn to love and accept me, warts and all. I knew it wasn't going to be easy, but it was a start when these two gorgeous men loved me.

That acceptance had helped, but several hours later, as I pretended to watch the movie Bailey had selected, I couldn't figure out how to talk about what was on my mind.

I stretched out a little more, moving my head that was resting in Jake's lap and my legs to drape a little more over Bailey's thighs. His hand automatically stroked over my stump, as if to soothe me. At times I wondered if he was even aware how often he touched my damaged leg. Whenever I chose not to wear my prosthesis about the house, he'd always find a way to have my legs over his thighs so he could caress me. In the beginning, it had weirded me out, but now I was so used to his touch it was as familiar as my own.

Jake also liked to touch. He was, however, more about making sure I was considered when we made love or went to the playroom so that I could manage without looking foolish. Those simple things showed me more than any declaration that they accepted me. Now I just needed to prove it to the doubting-Thomas inside my head!

Easy!

Chapter Twenty-Four

*J*ake

*S*am continued to fidget throughout the movie, and Bailey glanced at me several times with a worried look in his eyes. He remained silent and stroked Sam's legs. I was happy to note the swelling and redness had all but disappeared with rest and a little TLC.

I gave Bailey a reassuring wink, even though I was a little at a loss to figure out what was playing on Sam's mind. I'd noticed the other night he'd had what looked like an intense conversation with Bailey while I'd been serving a customer, but neither man had mentioned what it had been about. I'd wanted to question Bailey, but when he'd not been forthcoming, I'd decided to let it be. Now, I wasn't so sure that had been a wise decision.

I'd already pushed Sam to relax and do nothing until he had to return to work. To make sure that happened, I'd extended my holiday to ensure he did as he was told. And he had, fully embracing the time we spent just hanging out together.

With his leg initially giving him so much trouble, I'd avoided mentioning going to the playroom. Instead I'd lavished attention on both men in our bed. The memory of what we'd done this morning floated into my head. Bailey had lovingly sucked on Sam's cock while he sucked Bailey's. I'd watched them as I'd stroked myself to orgasm, spraying them both. They'd then licked each other clean before giving me a filthy kiss. The sight of them together, pleasuring each other, was fast becoming one of my most favourite pastimes. Heat spread to my groin and my cock started to take notice of where my head had gone, and Sam shifted so he could look up at me.

"I don't think you're paying attention to Hannibal. And if you are, Bailey and I are in serious trouble." He chuckled and glanced at Bailey, grinning when all he did was raise his brows at the pair of us. "Jake's cock is trying to poke a hole in my neck," Sam explained.

"I'm sure Sir was just enjoying your *head* resting in his lap," Bailey said with amusement.

I tutted at them both playfully. "I was thinking about this morning." Both men groaned, but only Sam's hand moved towards his groin. "Where do you think you're putting that hand?"

Sam huffed, said hand dropping straight back to the sofa and he shifted his gaze back to the telly. I stroked my hand over his silky hair as he started to fidget again and reminded me about my concerns. "Sammy?"

He reluctantly looked back up at me, and I saw resignation in his eyes, and if I wasn't mistaken, trepidation too. "Do you want to talk about what's bothering you?"

He glanced over at Bailey, who had gone completely still. "Did you say something?" Sam accused.

Bailey met Sam's angry glare. "No."

Sam visibly relaxed. "Sorry, I don't know why I asked that. I know you wouldn't say anything."

Bailey shrugged, his face not giving a lot away as Sam looked at me. "Bailey suggested I think about how you both could prove how much…you love me," he muttered the last part, so I had to strain to hear him.

"Okay, and what did you come up with?" I held my breath, waiting to see what his answer would be. I prayed hard it had nothing to do with the appointment I'd insisted he make at the prosthetic clinic.

His face became flushed as his eyelashes lowered to shield his eyes from me, my stomach lurching unpleasantly. "I was thinking that you and Bailey could be my masters at the next planned puppy night at the bar."

The air left my chest noisily. "Fuck, seriously? I love that idea. Me and Bailey as your masters, bring it. When's the next puppy play night?" Excitement buzzed through me, and for a second, my pulse deafened me as it roared in my ears.

"—Saturday of the month. I wasn't going to mention it…but well now…" Sam trailed off, looking uncertain.

"Tomorrow?" I questioned in a panic, thinking about the plans I'd made for Sunday with my parents that I'd not yet mentioned.

"No, the last Saturday of next month, Sir," Bailey replied, his brows arching as he gave me a questioning look.

"Oh, that's perfect because I was meaning to mention that I invited my parents around for Sunday lunch this weekend." If I'd said I was straight and into women I still don't think either man would have looked half as stunned as they did right then.

I shifted, warmth starting to heat my face uncomfortably

Sam was the first to recover. He sat up, dropping his legs over the edge of the sofa as he twisted his body towards me. "What the fuck?" His hands ran through his hair and his eyes grew wider. "Did you tell them about…us?"

"Of course, have I not mentioned this?" I frowned at the two blank faces. Then recalled the day I came home and found Sam and Bailey in the playroom. *Shit*. Had what had happened derailed any type of conversation afterwards? I racked my brains, coming up blank.

I sighed at my own lack and rubbed at my face. "I love you both. I'm not going to hide either of you. My parents love me, and I want them to love you pair too. I told my father about you both months ago, and I went to visit my mother after I'd let my father explain." The heat in my face increased as Sam's expression morphed into a look of disbelief and Bailey shifted closer to him, looking accusingly over his shoulder.

"In my defence, it was the day I came home and you both were in the playroom," I gritted out, feeling more than a little defensive.

"Sir, I call bullshit. You've had *months* to tell us. And you've since organised for them to come here, so you've had ample time to talk about this!" Bailey didn't pull his punches, and I flinched at the accusation.

He was right, of course. I'd had months and I had no excuse. "I apologise. Do you want me to ring my parents and tell them Sunday is off?"

"Don't you dare! It will look like we don't want to meet them." Sam's voice sounded strained as he leant back against Bailey as if seeking support.

Bailey clasped his arms around his waist and held him, but I could see the worried lines appearing around his eyes and mouth. "They'll love you, Sammy," Bailey crooned in Sam's ear.

"That will be a first. No parent has ever loved me," Sam muttered under his breath, but loud enough that we both heard him.

I shifted so that I could wrap my arms around both men and pulled them closer, cushioning Sam between Bailey and me. "My parents aren't fools. They'll see how wonderful you are."

"What if they don't?" There was genuine fear in Sam's voice as he spoke.

I placed my chin on top of his head and held him tighter. "Then they'll find they won't be welcome in this house. You and Bailey, that's what's most important to me. If my parents don't like it, then tough. I love you both. Nothing is going to change that." I hoped they'd listen and hear me because I meant every word.

***

Two days later I opened my front door to greet my parents, feeling frazzled after spending the last couple of days trying to placate both men. I prayed that I hadn't made a huge mistake.

Sam had not slept a wink the night before and was snapping at me every five minutes.

Then there was Bailey, fussing and panicking over the food in the kitchen. I'd almost been tempted to ring my parents to cancel. Only the huge effort both men had gone to for today had stopped me.

I plastered a smile to my face, hoping my parents couldn't tell how frazzled I was. "It's great to see you both, I'm glad you could come." I shook my father's hand and kissed my mother's cheek.

There was a familiar scent of Chanel, her favourite perfume, and if I weren't mistaken, she'd been to the hairdressers to have her roots touched up. As a natural blonde, she preferred to hide the few greys she had. She was vain and admitted it. No matter how many times my father and I told her she didn't look sixty, she still spent an age maintaining her appearance. The suit was mauve and matched the shoes and handbag she carried. It fitted her trim body, which was subjected to several weekly workouts.

She, unfortunately, looked like she was going for dinner at The Savoy rather than Sunday lunch at her son's home. I swallowed a sigh, knowing she'd come dressed to impress my men. My father, thankfully, looked a little less formal in beige slacks and a cream polo shirt with his Henley jacket left undone. He carried a bag that clinked, and I offered to take it.

"Oh, what is that delicious smell?" my mother asked as she stepped past me and headed straight for the stairs.

"Bailey decided to try out this new blackberry and plum sauce recipe he found that goes with the leg of lamb he's cooking." I wasn't sure she even heard me, not even pausing as she carried on up the stairs.

My father patted my arm after shutting the door behind him. "Don't worry, she's just as nervous as you. She'll relax once we get her tipsy," he assured me.

"I bloody hope so. I'm not sure why I thought this was a good idea."

My father's chuckle was drowned out by Sam's squeal. I ran for the stairs and was a panting, sweating mess as I crested the top to find my mother hugging Sam so tight his face was turning an alarming shade of red. Bailey stood watching, his mouth hanging open.

I ignored the sound of my Father coming up the stairs behind me. "Mum, whatever are you doing to Sam? You need to stop before he passes out."

"I'm just giving your boy a hug." She gave Sam a big smile, rubbing at his arms before she finally released him and turned her attention to Bailey. "What a big man you are. You're a little older than my Jakey, aren't you?" As she spoke, she walked towards Bailey, who physically braced as her arms came out to give him the same hard hug she'd given Sam.

I bit my lower lip to stop the laughter escaping at the flustered look on Bailey's face and the relieved look on Sam's. "The lady trying to squeeze you to death is my mother, Violet, and this is my father, Hubert."

I wasn't sure if either man heard me, but right then, I couldn't have cared less as I wanted to hug my mother for the easy display of affection she'd shown both men. "Anyone like a glass of wine?"

"Me please, and make it large," Sam asked, his gaze never moving from my mother.

"Yes please, son, we got an Uber so we could have some wine with...what smells like a glorious dinner," Father said, his face as bemused as Bailey's.

"I'll help."

Sam didn't give me time to answer as he walked over to the counter where I'd left the opened red wine, giving it a chance to breathe. It was one my parents liked, and I was pretty sure it was also in the bag I still held. I put it on the counter and noticed my hands were shaking.

I glanced back to Bailey and my mother and shook my head. "Mum, you can release Bailey now." I caught Bailey's relieved expression and again had to bite my lower lip to stop from laughing.

Bailey, now free, rushed back over to the simmering pots, casting worried glances at my mother every now and again, like she might attack him with another hug.

To distract my mother, I gave her a glass of wine and encouraged her and my father to sit at the table. I chatted about the trip to Scotland and distracted everyone enough that they all appeared to settle and take a breath.

By the time we were all seated at the table eating, the tension in the room had eased. Both Sam and Bailey no longer looked like they were about to snap, and they were both flushed from the praise and the wine they'd consumed. A warm glow filled my chest as my parents took the time to get to know both men.

Emotions swam through me as I watched Sam become animated as she spoke with my mother about his job. And Bailey spent some time talking with my father about his time in the army. The afternoon sun set across the sky as we moved to sit on the sofas. I positioned Sam and Bailey on either side of me, neither appearing concerned when my parents sat opposite, smiling at the three of us.

"I hope when you come to our house for dinner next, I can match the magnificent meal you made Bailey," said my mother.

"I helped," Sam said, grinning tipsily at everyone.

"I'm sure you can more than match my cooking skills. I can give you the web addresses I've been using. They have some fabulous ideas on there," Bailey offered.

I sank back into the cushions and slung my arms over the back of the sofa, touching both men. I caught them staring briefly at me out of the corner of my eyes as I stroked their hair. They shifted their attention back to my parents, but not before they relaxed beside me.

The heat and scent of them surrounded me and the love I wasn't afraid to acknowledge filled me from top to bottom, leaving me full to capacity. Life just couldn't get any better than this. Three was the magic number!

Epilogue

Bailey

My palms were sweaty as I rubbed them down the side of my leather trousers, waiting for Sam to reappear from the changing room. *What was taking him so long? Should I go and help him?*

I shook my head. He'd been insistent the last couple of times we'd come to the bar on the puppy nights that he could get himself ready.

"He'll be out when he's ready," Jake murmured next to my ear, to be heard over the music playing in the background and the people talking around us.

Puppy play evenings at the bar had become very popular, or so it seemed the last couple of times we'd come. The place had been packed, and Nathan had said they'd sold out of tickets for the events so fast he'd added a couple more dates to the calendar so people didn't miss out.

I glanced nervously at Jake. "I know, Sir. I'm just excited to take him up on the stage. I hate that Nathan had to introduce a booking system, so you have to book in advance to spend time up there. If Sam hadn't faffed so much, we'd have not been left with the last

239

slot, which also happens to be the first slot. You know Sam likes to pimp and preen in the changing room. If he doesn't hurry, we'll hardly get any time up there."

The whininess in my voice got an arched brow from Jake, even as he chuckled.

"My sweet sub, so eager to display our pup." Jake's hand slid down my back until it reached my arse, and he gave me a hard squeeze. I groaned at the heat that flared to life. Jake had caned me to orgasm the day before and the red welts were still present.

"Do you need me to distract you until Pup returns?" The pressure on my arse increased, and my groan became a whimper as my cock plumped to strain against the leather front of my trousers.

It might be the middle of February and cold enough to freeze the balls off a brass monkey outside, but right then, I felt like I was in the tropics. And okay, that might have had something to do with the anticipation and desire flowing through me like hot lava. Jake's touch burned.

Coming to the bar to play and display our pup was special, but with Jake's possessive touch it took things to a whole new level tonight. On the whole, these nights had become more than I could ever have imagined. We got to watch Sam glow with sheer joy under the praise and attention from other masters, but I was the one who then got to hold Sam's lead and give him what he'd always wanted: me being his master. It was a heady combination when Jake was added into the mix.

Jake's easy acceptance of me doing this for Sam made it perfect. Jake understood I didn't want to be dominant in our relationship. No, what I did for Sam was something different. It affirmed the love I felt for him and gave him a part of a long-held dream he'd had before Jake. Although our dreams had shifted and reformed into something else, the part that Sam had yearned for had remained. So we'd all talked about it, and when we'd come that first night back in October, it had set the scene for our following play dates at the bar. Then afterwards, Jake took us home and laid claim to us both.

It worked for all of us, and the fact it gave Sam a newfound confidence and acceptance that he was indeed loveable, was the icing on a very happy cake.

"I don't think my distraction is working," Jake whispered in my ear. His warm breath left my ear tingling, and I glanced at him, offering up my lips for a kiss.

He obliged, his mouth rubbing sensually against mine. As much as I loved these one on one kisses, the three-way kisses were what I hungered for. His tongue swept over the seam of my lips and I opened as he deepened the kiss. His chest pushed against me and the hand not holding my arse gripped the back of my neck in a possessive hold.

I mewled into his mouth, my body responding to his hungry desire. I resisted thrusting my hips, not wanting to gain a punishment, knowing how Jake would use my need against me. The pressure on my arse increased before he pinched playfully.

"Oh, Sir, oh please, harder," I begged unashamedly.

"I promise I'll give you everything you need when we get home."

He gave me another hard pinch, and my eyes closed as the sensations bled into each other.

"Open your eyes sub, you're missing seeing our pup make an entrance." Jake chuckled darkly as his fingers continued to play as my eyes slitted open with difficulty. I exhaled at the wave of lust that left me breathless and eager.

Sam was on all fours, his head tilted alluringly to one side. His mask tonight was dark red and matched the lead and collar he had clasped between his teeth, and the tail he wore. They were the gifts I'd given him for Christmas. I'd contacted the company that had made his other mask and commissioned new ones as a surprise. They'd also made two new tails, a lead, and a collar that had all our names on it.

He moved towards us with a confidence that was breath-taking as he eyed me and Jake with love and adoration. His new tail moved seductively behind him and his cock swayed with excitement. To me, he'd never looked sexier or more alluring.

***

${\mathcal{S}}$am

I inhaled the heady scent of leather and sex as I entered the bar, searching the busy area for my men. The place was decorated for Valentine's Day. My back twinged remembering how long it had taken to string up all the multicoloured fairy lights around the large bar, and love hearts that hung them from every available place me and Ferron could find.

Nathan had bitched a little about the cost, but as I eyed the room and watched the flickering lights dance off all the men dressed as puppies, I couldn't help but think it had been worth it.

When my gaze landed on the two men stood by the far side of the bar, my whole body quivered. Jake's possessive hold on Bailey was doing a number on him. Bailey was flushed and his chest was moving rapidly, and I wondered what Jake was doing with his other hand as Bailey shut his eyes and his mouth opened. I chuckled when Jake whispered something to Bailey and his eyes slitted open and he stared directly at me. My heart leapt with joy as both men's faces filled with love.

How is this my life? *It is, now get your arse over to your men.*

Nervous energy made it hard to focus as I moved across the floor on my hands and knees towards both men, a smile spreading over my face. My teeth clamped a little tighter around the lead and collar I'd placed between my lips before I'd left the changing room.

Most of the puppies that came to play were normally already dressed in their gear when they arrived. I'd figured out the first night, with my leg being the way it was, that it was a little more difficult for me to do so. So I'd conceded to use the changing room that was on offer, but only after I'd had a little pity-party.

Bailey had talked some sense into me and had come into the changing room to help me change. I'd been pleased to note that I wasn't the only one choosing to use it. Not that I'd made eye contact with anyone as Bailey had undressed and redressed me. No, that had taken another couple of visits, but I was okay with it now. So much so, I didn't care who looked at me anymore.

What had surprised me was the praise I'd received from puppies and masters alike when I'd been displayed on the stage. There'd been no negative reaction, not that I thought for one minute Jake and Bailey would have tolerated that. They tended to stay close to show whoever chose to look that I was with them, and that had helped more than anything to alleviate my anxieties.

The first night, with Jake and Bailey's love and support, I'd eventually managed to gain the right headspace to play and let go. And boy had it been fun with both my men. Bailey had taken me up on the stage and encouraged me to sit in his lap so he could pet me. I'd come all over his leather trousers and gained a spanking from Jake that had been so worth it.

These nights had given me back a little of what I'd lost when the shrapnel and following infection had taken my leg. But the men waiting for me, they'd given me a whole lot more; unconditional love, and that was priceless.

***

$\mathcal{J}$ake

Emotions flashed over Sam's face as he moved over the floor with grace and a confident air that caused my body to react. Then the fucker gave me one of those sexy grins around the lead and collar clasped between his teeth. Fuck, I wanted to take both men home and show them just how much I loved them.

My grip on Bailey's neck increased and he moaned. I nuzzled into the scented skin at the side of his neck, not once taking my gaze off the man coming towards us. The bar seemed to fade away. "Look at how confident he is for his master," I whispered against Bailey's flesh, receiving a whole-body shudder. "When we leave tonight, I think we might need to re-enact the first time Pup rode your cock."

"Oh, to the gods...please, Sir, I'm going to come if you carry on," Bailey gasped, his body moving restlessly against mine.

Sam quirked his head as he continued towards us. His gaze moved to Bailey's crotch and I imagined the bulge that Bailey would be sporting right now. Sam licked at his lips and his eyes darkened. I couldn't see his cheeks, but I'd bet they were as flushed as his neck and bare chest.

"I think Pup wants to use you as a suck toy. Should I let him? Should I pull your cock out so you can show everyone what a good master you are to our pup. I'm sure he'd love to nibble on all that hard flesh. Taste you on his tongue, then maybe—"

Bailey froze for long seconds in my arms, a cry of alarm leaving his lips.

"Oh, sub, did you come without permission. Were you disobedient?" I didn't conceal my glee. Both Sam and Bailey loved it when I talked dirty to them, both finding it equally hard to not come when I pushed, like now.

He sagged and his trembling body pressed more firmly against me. "I'm sorry, Sir," Bailey gasped as Sam reached us.

"Do you want to lick your master clean, Pup?" I asked, just loud enough for Sam to hear.

His eyes glowed in the mask as he nodded eagerly and dropped the collar and lead on the floor. Powerful desire, that only seemed to increase as the months went by, flared to life, leaving me cursing that we weren't at home so I could do everything I wanted. I gritted my teeth, making my jaw bounce as I reminded myself I could do whatever I wanted because these men were mine. And I was going to make sure it stayed that way.

Nerves danced in my belly at thoughts of the two boxes that were sat in my briefcase ready for the right moment. Would they say yes?

I looked from one man to another and my nerves settled at the love I could see. A wicked smile spread over my face. This was definitely only the beginning.

The End... but not really as you'll find the boys pop up in other books in this series and The Playroom, The App and possibly others.

If you enjoyed this book, read on for a bonus excerpt from Reluctant Billionaire (book two) Billionaire's Playground.

PROLOGUE

Brett

As I slipped into the back of the Uber, I groaned aloud. The guy eyed me in the rear-view mirror but said nothing as he merged with the traffic to take me to the Flamingo Bar.

I loved Luke with all my heart, as a friend, but I'd admitted to myself I was jealous of what he had with Scott. They were so happy together, and this engagement party, though it filled me with utter joy for my best friend, left me green with envy. I'd always thought it would be me getting engaged first.

How did that turn out?

A stab of hurt pierced my heart and I rubbed at the centre of my chest. Ever since Nigel had cheated on me, then dumped me after five years being together, I'd admit to being floored. His comment that 'I was too out there for him' left me cold when I'd only experimented to keep things spiced up between us.

Luke had pointed out the fact that Nigel was a spineless dick, who'd shown his true colours in the end. That I'm a bloody doctor of psychology says I should have noticed how bad things had become between us. But no, I'd buried my head in the sand, to the point where I lost sight of what was happening in my own life.

Months had passed, and I was still struggling to get past it. The unsettling reality is that I was more upset by the fact I'd been duped than by Nigel dumping me.

I stared out of the window at the darkening sky and tried to distract myself with thoughts of what I'd find at this new kink bar. I'd tried many things over the years, hoping to keep Nigel interested, but nothing seemed to hold my attention for more than a few months before I'd be looking for something different to try.

You're supposed to be thinking about something other than Nigel!

The voice of reason did little to help settle my clenching gut, and by the time the car pulled up outside the large, converted warehouse, my mood had plummeted.

The warehouse was huge, consisting of three floors and an underground car park for patrons. The ground floor was a BDSM club called The Playroom that I'd never been in, but I was told it was a popular place for those interested in BDSM.

It was the next floor where I was headed. The Flamingo Bar was the newly refurbished part of the large warehouse. It was split into two, with a new restaurant in the La Trattoria Di Amore franchise and the kink bar. Carl, the head chef of the restaurant, was also the co-owner of the club below and the bar with Nathan. I'd not met either man as yet, though I'd heard good things about both of them from Luke and Scott.

Scott was the head waiter in the Flamingo Bar restaurant, and was also Luke's boy, which is why they'd decided to use this venue. The bar was geared to the lighter side of kink, Daddy kink, puppy/kitty play, age play, and any other kind of play imaginable.

In the empty lift, I leant back against the wall and inhaled a breath, then another, to help centre myself. I eyed my skinny trousers in deep brown that matched my snug-fitting jacket. The burnt orange shirt I'd paired it with was also fitted, and I sucked in my stomach when it poked out over my belt.

The door opened, and I was distracted from my weight gain by the scent of Italian food and expensive colognes. The room was an eclectic mix of reclaimed wood fittings and modern fixtures. The handcrafted bar was beautiful, as were the booths that lined the walls, which also looked as if they'd been handcrafted. The dimmed lights that hung from recycled chains had different coloured glass bottles as shades, which cast coloured light over the tables in the booths.

"There you are, I thought you'd got lost," Luke exclaimed as he rushed towards me, looking more than a little flustered.

"Now, you know I like to make an entrance, honey." I puckered up my lips, and Luke rolled his eyes but gave in and pressed a quick, platonic kiss to my lips.

"Hey, what's this? I turn my back on you for two minutes and already you're kissing other men." Scott's eyes gleamed as he threaded his arm through Luke's and beamed at me, not looking in the least bit upset.

I offered my lips to him, "I'll happily give you a kiss too."

As he went to step forward, Luke held him back. "Nope, not happening. You kiss his sweet lips and you might get second thoughts about our engagement."

"As if, Daddy," Scott mock-whispered back, looking about to check no one was close.

Luke was still reasonably new to the Daddy scene, and though Scott wasn't, he was always mindful not to out Luke in front of his friends and work colleagues.

"Scott, have you got a moment? I need you to check you're happy with... something," asked a pretty guy dressed in a black shirt with pink flamingos on it.

"What's this about? You promised me you weren't going to be doing any work-related stuff tonight." Luke's brow furrowed as his gaze moved between the two men. "What gives Theo?"

"Luke, it's a secret," Scott stated in an exasperated tone as he rolled his eyes at Theo.

I chuckled when Luke got a twinkle in his eyes as he whispered something into Scott's ear, making his boy's cheeks fill with a flare of pink. Scott kissed his cheek before walking off with the other man.

"He looks so happy. I'm happy for you both." I glanced at Luke as he turned to stare at me.

"I know this is hard for you after—"

"Do not mention he who shall remain nameless. We're supposed to be having a good time." I swept my gaze around the bar before landing back on Luke. "Maybe I'll meet the man of my dreams tonight."

He laughed. "You know almost everyone that is coming tonight. Is there something you want to tell me?"

"Nope, but hope springs eternal." I sounded sad even to my own ears, so I offered him an extra bright smile, knowing it wouldn't fool him for a second but I had to try.

"I'm told Sam, the head barman, makes a killer cocktail. Let's go get one." Luke's eyes said that he was letting it go for tonight, but that he'd be having words with me at some point.

I threaded my arm through his and we went to the bar. He was right, Sam did make a killer cocktail. He was also a cute guy who liked to flirt. It didn't hurt my ego at all when he chatted me up and gave me a flirty wink before he went to serve someone else.

By the second cocktail, and having not eaten, I was starting to feel the nice floaty alcohol effects. I excused myself to use the bathroom, and on my return, Luke was no longer stood at the bar, but was talking to a number of men, including...Griffin Hudson, *shit.*

I got the feeling Griffin, who was exceedingly private, might find it difficult to see me after his last visit to my office. It happened from time to time when I was out and bumped into a client.

Unable to avoid the situation, I headed straight to the group of men. Walking up behind Luke, I wrapped my arm through his, giving everyone a bright smile. It was only then that I got a full look at the man stood next to Griffin's boyfriend Charlie. *Holy fuck!*

The wattage of my smile increased as my gaze travelled up his willowy frame. Thigh-length black leather boots were paired with super-skinny black jeans that made his legs appear as if they went on forever. The black fitted shirt had panelled mesh sides to show off his gorgeous body and made my mouth water. He was pretty, with blue-grey flecked eyes that showed a hint of uncertainty.

"Hello, sweetie, and who might you be?" I cooed.

Luke rolled his eyes and Griffin coughed, while the nameless man's face gained a beautiful rosy glow to it. His eyelashes lowered, and when he remained silent, I got the distinct impression that I might have embarrassed him.

Charlie nudged the man not so subtly and huffed as Griffin coughed again. "Hi, I'm Charlie. This is Guy, my best friend. And you are?"

I gave them both a big grin as I offered my manicured hand to Guy. "I'm Brett Louden, Luke's best friend...and Griffin's..."

I hesitated as Griffin stiffened next to Charlie. There was an awkward silence as I continued to hold Guy's hand, until I noticed Luke eyeing me. I reluctantly let go when Charlie spoke.

"It's nice to meet you, Brett, but I could really do with a drink. Guy, do you want a drink? Luke, Brett? Griffin and I can go to the bar."

Once Charlie had everyone's orders, they walked towards the bar, disappearing in the crowd. Luke glanced between me and Guy before he came up with some lame excuse and left too.

"How long have you been friends with Charlie?" I asked after searching for something to say to break the sudden tension rolling off Guy.

His face brightened. "Oh, since I started uni. We met in halls and ended up sharing a room. That was up until recently, he's moved in with Griffin now. But it's not too bad as we're in our final year." His slim shoulders shrugged as he glanced towards the bar, as if willing Charlie to reappear.

"That's how I met Luke. We lived together for four years." I wanted to slap my head when Guy's eyes widened and he looked over to where Luke stood with his arm draped over Scott's shoulders. A look of disappointment flittered over his face before his head moved and he looked back at me.

"Just as friend's, Guy, Luke is the brother I never had," I clarified, hoping I was reading him right.

When his lips moved into a beautiful smile, my heart thudded against my ribs. "Oh, right. You weren't ever an item?" he asked hesitantly.

"No, we kissed a couple of times when we were drunk." I chuckled. "It lacked any chemistry."

His eyes sparkled with humour. "That was like me and Charlie."

I linked my arm through his and gave him a sexy wink. "Then we already have lots in common. You want to find out what else we might have in common?"

Guy blushed but nodded as Charlie returned with our drinks.

Three hours later, feeling the effects of Guy's undivided attention and several cocktails, I pressed him up against the wall by the packed dance floor and kissed him.

His lips were soft, and he tasted of sweet alcohol as he allowed me to deepen and control the kiss. His slim body pressed firmly against mine, and his body's reaction became obvious as his cock pressed against my hip bone. The kiss ended all too quickly, when Charlie came to see if Guy was ready to leave.

Tempted to ask him back to mine, I instead offered him my number. After we'd exchanged digits, he left, and I went to the bathroom to make myself decent before I went to find Luke.

In the bathroom I couldn't resist sending Guy a text.

Thank you for making the evening extra special. I hope we can do this again soon, Brett x

I read it twice before I hit send. A smile plastered to my face, I went to find Luke, feeling the first flare of real happiness in months.

Six days later, the spark of happiness I'd felt at Luke and Scott's engagement party had fled. Guy hadn't answered my text, or the one I'd sent him three days earlier asking if he'd like to go out on a date.

I sighed and glanced at my phone, switching it to silent and putting it in my desk drawer before my next client arrived. I had a firm no phone rule in my office and that also applied to me. I hated that I'd broken the rule over the last three days, waiting like an idiot for Guy to reply. I'd gone over the evening, and I couldn't figure out why the radio silence. I'd reached out to Griffin to check nothing had happened to Guy. When he'd come back saying Guy was fine, my heart had sunk.

No more. It stops now!

It was his loss if he couldn't see what a great catch I was.

Really, then why are you single?
Oh, shut up!

About the author

Hi all,

My name is Jayne and I live in the Isle of Man. A tiny place in the Irish sea. It's an island steeped in folklore and history and just begs to have stories written about it, and one of my true inspirations.

I've been happily married for over 25 years to a wonderfully complicated man, and I have a wonderful daughter with two very young grandbabies. I am also an identical twin, so if you see me, check, as it may not be me.

I've written an eclectic mix of books, mainly contemporary gay romance with a paranormal twist, daddy kink, fake boyfriends, out for you and enemies to lovers, along with many other tropes. All of my series are listed if you want to find other books to read. They are all on Amazon and in KU.

If you would like to give me any feedback or just have any questions, go ahead and friend me on Facebook, and I would be happy to answer anything. Well, almost anything. I hope you enjoyed this book as it was a little different for me. If you would also like to leave a review, then I would love to read your thoughts.

Thank you for taking the time to be part of my dream.